PROMISED
LAND

Promised Land

Alan Marcus

ISBN-13: 978-0-9629909-4-6

© 2016 Other Shores Press. Carmel, CA

Please address all queries, comments, and requests
for further information to
OtherShorePress@prodigy.net

PROMISED LAND

A Novel By

Alan Marcus

Remarks of Father Craft – Missionary to the Indians. 1889
Great Plains:

"Indians were not fools but men of keen intelligence… Reductions in rations increased fears. Census takers made grave mistakes, counted less than the real numbers; agents made false reports of prosperity that did not exist… It is not to be wondered that they finally came to believe in a Messiah whom they at first doubted, and listened to every deceiver who promised hope…

"Interested whites took advantage of this state and howled for troops; the army protested their false statements but were required to go to the scene of supposed dangers… Persuaded by some whites that their entire destruction was aimed at, the Indians ran away in fear and despair…"

Remarks of a Sioux Chief:

"When I was a boy, the Sioux owned the world. The sun rose and set in their land. They sent ten thousand horsemen to battle. Where are the warriors today? Who slew them? Where are our lands? Who owns them? Is it wrong for me to love my own? Wicked in me because my skin is red; because I am a Sioux, because I was born where my father lived; because I would die for my own people……"

The Captain

Thanksgiving Day, 1890, Pine Ridge Reservation, South Dakota.

Savages, Savages.

When the Colonel called me to his office, I thought it was the usual thing, and I already had in mind who I would take with me out on patrol this time; Bates, Yollison, the three Pah-Utes boys we had, and the two young Sioux back from Carlisle. But I was mad just the same. Cold as midnight out, frost on the ground, and us just back from five days scouting southwest of Rushville. If you think autumn in South Dakota is nothing but pretty snowscapes, you've never lived there. But I suppose I'm not used to it – the Indians bear up alright, and my God, what they wear wouldn't keep a baby duck properly sheltered.

Anyway when I came in and saluted, with a list all made up in my mind, there was the Colonel, and sitting next to him, Boyer, the agent; also a fat man name Bergman, one of the ranchers in the county. All three men looked grim as hell.

"Delaney," says the Colonel, "I want you to take a detail of men, line 'em up in formation side of the Government corral. I want 'em there two o'clock, and I want 'em with rifles loaded."

"A detail?" Bergman said. "With fifteen hundred of those savages coming in for their ration, and the war paint barely rubbed off for only this one day, to fool us into thinking peace is their intention!"

"Our aim is to prevent bloodshed, not bring on violence; and I don't believe anything's going to happen."

"We have a right to demand protection, Colonel," says Bergman. "As soldiers you have a duty to the ranchers of the whole country."

"I don't think there's anything to worry about," says the Colonel. Then Boyer, the agent, put his two cents in. He's a skinny little man, not a bad sort, but ever since the trouble started last year, all those rumors and Indians moving all over the place, and fear rising, and ugliness growing in everybody, whites and Indians alike, he's been out of his depth. He just weren't ever made for crises.

"Perhaps if we just trust Colonel Donaldson," he says to Bergman, "Why I'm sure everything, yes, and."

"The point is," Bergman cried, "these blasted Indians think they got everything coming to them. Sure, hundreds of thousands of dollars a year to keep them in food and clothes; all that range land they got, they're just wasting it! You know as well as I, the Government pays $4.75 a piece for their blankets, and just as much for every other little whatnot too, and all you have to do is ride over to Chamberlain or Rushville soon's they get an issue – clothes, hats, ropes, they sell it all and then lie about it and beg for more. They got twice as much reservation land right now as they should have."

"The problem," says Boyer, "is one of adjustment."

"Adjustment hell!" Bergman shouted, and rushed out of the office. Boyer rushed after him.

So Colonel Donaldson and I were left looking at each other. I knew well enough what he was thinking; ever since I'd been sent out to Pine Ridge from Omaha, I'd watched him trying to make sense out of a situation as tangled and ornery as any that could be imagined. Maintain order, and carry out Government directives – that was the assignment. But which order, and which agency of Government? Sure, there were thousands of Indians scattered over several hundred miles on these two big reservations at Rosebud and Pine Ridge, and hundreds of white settlers living within reach. But what was happening now didn't just spring up overnight; it must've started back when all these Sioux were given these lands for the first time. Or may be back further even, before Custer, when they had the Black Hills all to themselves. And now with the Indian Department shouting one thing, and the Army yelling for another, and ranchers and prospectors all trying to get their licks in, and not one man in a thousand that really understands the Indians – how in blazes can you make any sense out of it?

"Delaney," the Colonel says and sighs. "There's over two thousand Indians drawing their cattle this afternoon, but I'm banking on their being hungry enough to concentrate on rations and nothing else. All these hotheads and alarm-carousers like Bergman notwithstanding............."

Bergman! Wasn't it him who started the panic back last month, bringing those painted horses he says he found near his place, parading them down the street here till everyone was making a great scared run for Rushville ten miles away, thinking the Sioux were gathering for a bloody attack on the Agency. But nothing happened, rumors and more rumors, and that's all. I haven't been out here long enough to start giving advice, but if all these damn Sioux are really as pestiferous as everyone says, why not go after them instead of waiting around here like this with our troops scattered in strength all up and down South Dakota? Well, the Colonel says wait, and General Fleming, and the whole goddamn war department too. But if it was up to Lawrence P. Delaney, Esquire...

"That's all, Delaney," the Colonel says, breaking in on me. "See you this afternoon. And happy Thanksgiving Day."

Happy Thanksgiving! Yeah, you should've seen it. The most sickening day in a way I ever lived through in all my life. All those Indians out there on that plain, standing still in freezing cold wind, some of them must've come from over a hundred miles. And those agency clerks, bawling out the names of the head men in each hand, and then the wooden padlock each time moving back, and one lousy scrawny steer rushing out, hunted and chased and roped all over the plains by those young men on their tiny horses. And meanwhile more steers coming out, more slipping and sliding and chasing, a great larruping over the plain. And the squaws and children trying to get out of the way of hooves and falling cattle, and white men gawking on, and me standing there foolish with my detail of soldiers.

I never saw anything more disgusting. Bergman is right in calling them savages, right there on that plain, men, women and children squatting around those thing steers, slaughtering them with knives. And afterwards hunched around a fallen animal all butchered and lying in pieces in its own hide to keep the sand out, and everybody eating everything raw, entrails, guts, everything. Oh it made some women vomit to watch. I swear you wouldn't believe aboriginals like that could still be living in a modern country like ours in the year 1890.

The Colonel had a big argument with Boyer, the agent, over it afterwards. Said it was a damn shame, making them chase their pitiful cattle, and all because someone was getting fat on the few dollars saved from the expense of a decent slaughtering. But Boyer said it was Washington who ordered it, because the hides had been promised, and if not, money from selling the hides could've paid for a decent slaughtering. But the Colonel got mad and snorted, and said look at the way they're eating those raw carcasses, and you'll find out why you had to send to Cheyenne and Omaha for troops to protect settlers. "I don't know who needs protecting from whom," the Colonel yelled, and Boyer got mad and him and the others, Bergman, White, and the other ranchers moved away, and after a while the windy plain was littered with festering leavings, and those hundreds of Indians began moving out, carrying bloody remains wrapped in hides.

When I got back to the barracks for Thanksgiving dinner, I couldn't hardly eat. Couldn't sleep well that night either. Kept dreaming of those silent aboriginals and their knives and that plain full of squatting mouths eating what they call the fifth quarter, the entrails and all. Some of our own scouts, too, you might think they were a little civilized at least, but what did they do? Rode in among their relatives and squatted down, reverting like all the rest, handling guts in their cupped naked hands.

There's no doubt about it. Savages is what they are – aboriginal savages!

A Wild Goose Chase

The next day I was finally all set to go on leave back to Omaha, because it was long due me, the Colonel had it already approved and I was looking forward to leaving Pine Ridge for a while, seeing what civilization looked like, when one of the enlisted men came for me, telling me the Colonel wanted to see me right away at the agency school.

My temper began boiling inside. Goddamn it, Donaldson knew how long I'd been waiting to go off, and my leave twice postponed already, on account of the Cheyenne's from the from the north, raiding away to the southwest country. A man can stand so long in this damn jittery Indian territory before he starts dreaming nightmares all the while.

But this time I was surprised. Colonel Donaldson was sitting there and a bunch of local men with him, the Indian agent, the ranchers committee, the Mayor of Rushville, and even General Fleming himself. The General must've ridden over in the night from Chadron, we hadn't even known he was planning to come here.

I stood at attention, but the Colonel waved me to a chair.

"Go ahead with what you were saying, Mr. Pickering," the Colonel said to a tall, bald-headed cattleman from the northwest part of the country.

"Well these four Sioux came by my place two nights ago, and they were painted up, they came to ask for water, and after some kind of meat, but when I asked them to be careful about the fire they looked at me with fierce faces and poured more logs on, and made threatening motions. My wife and I stayed with loaded rifles near the windows all night."

"I had a farmer tell me," said Father Broux, "that a friend of his rode down driving cattle near Rosebud recently and he saw a long line of picketed Indians on the slopes, all painted up, and signal fires at night."

"They're looking for trouble," cried a fat rancher (it was Bergman). "I say the Army ought to go out and drive them out of here. Plenty of room for them farther north anyway."

From Rushville, old Jeb Barker who runs a store there, said, "Indian came into my place the other day asking for gunpowder, and when I told him there weren't any, he drew his finger across his neck. Told me one day he'd be taking, not asking. His horse was scrubbed, but I could see the marks, it'd been painted recently, that's sure."

Then everyone began talking at once, saying how in Chadron last week the citizens got into such a panic, fearing the Sioux, they went and hid in a coal mine, and how some people reported thousands were gathering up north, holding the ghost-dances which were forbidden by the government, working themselves up into a painted lather. The memory of the terrible Sioux massacres on the Little Big Horn and earlier were still in people's minds, and now here they were again, planning to defy law it seems, and bolt off the reservation, hiding in the Badlands to the north, perhaps raiding and stealing horses, or worse. Everywhere you went you heard talk of the great Indian Messiah who was going to save the Indians. And that was the crux of the problem, Donaldson said, some bad Indians going around preaching they were prophets of a new savior, and working the bands up so that the chiefs wouldn't even come in from the reservation to discuss grievances any more.

"Discuss!" cried Bergman, and he seemed to be speaking for a lot of the others. "The time for talking is past! I'm telling you, General, if you'd only send an expedition out…"

"What we're trying to do is avoid bloodshed," said the Colonel, "not provoke it."

"Those Indians ain't got no backbone! Just send a few Gatling guns over to Rosebud, they'll scatter in no time. And what about the citizens who are living within reach, who's going to protect them if the government won't?"

"So far all we've got is rumors and incidents, - I intend to try and bring in a delegation from Porcupine Creek or White River and treat with them, not start bloodletting..."

Soon there was more yelling and shouting, and finally everyone left without coming to an agreement, and only I and the Colonel were sitting in the room, facing General Fleming.

"We could organize a force to march north into the reservation, try to disarm the Indians," said General Fleming. "But the orders from Washington are to wait. And besides, if they heard we were coming like that, there'd certainly be a bust-off. Buy trying to follow three thousand Indians into the Badlands, and the rest being scared into stampeding probably, and innocent settlers in their path... no, we'd better wait a while."

"But if we could get a dozen chiefs in from the hinterlands," the Colonel said. "To sit down and smoke with..."

"They won't come. This Messiah craze has them all worked up, and now with last summer's crop failure, and bungling of the census taking."

"Bungling? With two sets of figures going east, and somebody pocketing the difference?"

"If we had proof, Colonel. But these damn politicians are so bland and oily..."

"Then you'll let me send Delaney with Running Bear? Give us an authorization?"

"Even if they came in, I don't have authority from Washington to promise them a thing. And the Indian Department's set against it."

"But if they came in, General, there'd be time enough to worry about it."

"I don't know," said General Fleming. "I still think force is all they really understand."

The Colonel stood up. He's a small man, but when he talks authority stands out all over him. He's been in the Indian country for a long time, maybe fifteen years on and off. Talks Lakota, too. Nobody can sense what they're liable to do better than he.

"There's a tragedy in the making, General, and I submit it's better to try and prevent it than make excuses later about why it happened. If all the facts were out in the open, all of us'd be hanging our heads for the knowledge. But this way there's a chance and nothing's risked…"

"Except a few lives," the General says, and looks at me.

I felt a chill go through me. But I still didn't know what it was all about.

"Delaney," the Colonel says. "There's a Sioux Indian scout at Chadron, attached to Major Wheeler there, who's due up to Pine Ridge tomorrow. His name is Running Bear, he goes back onto the reservation to be with his people twice a year. One of the best and brightest scouts we've had. But the point is he's the son of Spotted Eagle, the chief of the Teton-Dakota band living up there now near White River. And old Spotted Eagle is one of the best Indian elders on the reservation. Never broken his word to the military, one of the eight signatories of the treaty of '87. If we could get him to come in, and bring some of the other chiefs in for a talk fest, I think the ice could be broken. Maybe we could nip this ghost-dance craze in the bud. If anyone can convince the old man, his son can because Running Bear has been with the soldiers, he knows the power of the military first-hand."

"But where do I come in, sir?" I asked.

"The Colonel's idea is for you to go out with this Indian with a warrant," said the General, "and assist him in making an arrest of whoever it is strutting around out there by White River, proclaiming himself God's Messiah and working the bands up into these damn ghost-dances, threatening to unite them and lead them off the reservation. If we send troops, there sure as hell be a fire fight, but all by himself Running Bear won't have the same authority to the chiefs as if he had a special officer emissary with him. So that's what the Colonel has in mind, a combination marshal and ambassador, because Spotted Eagle has got his people moving up White River away from the graze lands, and that means maybe he's fallen for all this ghost-dance craziness like the rest. If you could get to him in time..."

"It's not an order," the Colonel tells me. "But the Indians don't know you, Delaney, and right now they're apt to be soured on everyone they've seen before. So it's your own decision, go or not, and no prejudice either way, and with your own pick of posts when you come back."

"What about my leave to Omaha?"

"Leave? You'll get double the furlough and duty in Cheyenne if you want it. That's my promise."

"Think it over, Captain," the General said, and I stood up and saluted and walked out into the cold night air.

My first reaction was rage. Goddamn the Colonel! Those filthy savages with their knives eating raw flesh like gorillas, and he wants me to go out there alone, and with only a map knowledge of the reservation, dependent on one Sioux for my bearings, and not knowing hardly a single syllable of their impossible dialect, giving up my leave and maybe more than that for a regular wild goose chase. And asking me in such a way that doesn't leave any honorable escape batch either... I went and got my horse and rode into Rushville and sat down by the bar in Niobrara's café, drinking myself angry, and seeing those bloody Indians every time I looked into the glass.

I must've transferred a few quarts inside, and still not made up my mind when someone brushed against me outside just as I was leaving the place, a soldier, and he entering just as I was leaving so that the swinging door bumped up against me hard, and I fell plump on my tail in front of the motley group of onlookers, cackling at the sight of a Captain on his rear in Niobrara's. I don't know if it was the liquor or the doubt made me foolish, but I hauled up and called the man to account, and he turned around, smiling apology. He was tall and dark, and right away I noticed he wasn't enlisted in the ranks, his insignia showed him to be a volunteer scout of some kind. But then he must've been an Indian, and that was all I needed right then.

"No liquor's to be served this man," I yelled at Tiny who tends bar at Niobrara's. "That's according to Army regulations…"

"No, Captain," Tiny said. They were all laughing at me. Oh I felt a perfect fool, and meanwhile that damn Sioux dressed in Army khakis just stood there, at his perfect ease as tall as I was. But he must've been from General Fleming's entourage, I didn't recognize him as one of ours from Pine Ridge.

"Part of our damn trouble comes from serving these Indians whiskey. By God, if we find out about it…"

"Oh no, Captain," Tiny said, and I could've shot him dead on the spot. Everybody hooting at me, and my head beginning to swell, and that scout grinning and grinning, and the lights and the noise flashing all around.

So I went out. I rushed into the cold air and swung up and went for a ride to clear my head, and the more I rode the more I felt foolish for taking out my doubt and fear on that scout, looking like a spoiled kid in Niobrara's, and the more foolish I felt the more I sensed a decision hardening inside of me, and by the time I got back to the barracks, half frozen and stiff from the ride, I knew I was going to do what the Colonel asked.

To Keep the Peace

Seven a.m., next morning. The Colonel wasn't back from breakfast yet, so I sat down in the office, waiting. Then the door opened and who should come in? Sure, they very same one had gotten that crowd laughing at me last night in Niobraras.

He gave no sign of recognition though, just looked at me and away. But I knew it was the same man, there wasn't another scout that big in our whole unit. Besides, the General's entourage had taken off early before breakfast so's to get back to Chadron by nightfall. A helluva situation in a way, and what I wanted to do was to say something, break the ice a little but his manner didn't invite it. He just sat there with folded arms, looking out the window, and after about five minutes the Colonel came in, rubbing his hands, and stamping his boots out. Then we went through the farcical introduction.

"Captain Delaney," the Colonel says, "here's the man I was telling you about, Running Bear, from Major Wheeler's outpost at Chadron. I used to know his father, way back before I took a commission and joined myself to a wooden chair, growing fat over forms and fountain pens."

We shook hands.

Then Donaldson began talking quite seriously with the Sioux in Lakota dialect, using his hands, pointing to the map stretched out on his office desk. Which gave me a chance to take my bearings. One blizzard just over and another maybe on its way, and it was a hundred and twenty miles to White River if it was one. I'd been up there only once, with a training troop after I'd just arrived at Pine Ridge. But this was different, and if liquored been able to put some brag into me the night before, the facts staring at me from the Colonel's map sobered me up pretty quick on this cold morning.

"Delaney," the Colonel said. We've talked it over, and he thinks it might be best if you started off today, without waiting on official confirmation. I'll take responsibility for issuing a warrant myself, and you can draw supplies from Quarter-master.

You'll have to take several extra horses and travois because if there's as many Indians at White River as I think there are, giving gifts'll be your best entrée to them, and Running Bear thinks they may be planning to move out north any day. Time is the important thing, I want you up there as soon as possible.

"Excuse me, Colonel," the Indian says, and his voice was steady, the voice of a schooled Sioux, but all I remembered at the moment was yesterday afternoon, our 'civilized' scouts down on all fours eating those raw butchered steer quarters. "Excuse me," he says, "but they maybe not come so close all the way. Better you meet us with soldiers in one, two weeks' time. Perhaps make camp near Porcupine Creek, or Wounded Knee. Too many soldiers in agency, all the time with wheel guns. I think my father not come this far to agency."

The Colonel looked at me, stared at his sprawled map of Pine Ridge lying on the desk. Then he made some notations, beckoned to both of us. And right then and there he made a tracing, gave us a copy of alternate routes leading to a rendezvous spot about fifty miles southeast of White River, where the Yellow Creek joins the Cheyenne. And this was to be the stopping point for a force of troops which would leave either here, or General Fleming's headquarters in ten days' time, making camp at the marked coordinates.

"But the important thing," the Colonel said, "is that everybody understands why we're willing to treat with the Indians. Not because they've intimidated anyone, or scared the countryside, or because we're authorized to recompense them for promises broken; but because the duty of the Army here is to keep the peace, and I hope the Chiefs can be made to see how hopeless it'll be if they go off the reservation."

Then he looked out the window for a moment, and talked, more to himself in a musing kind of way, saying it was a long complicated mixture of events had brought things to this sorry state, with blame on both sides, though those who had more opportunity to understand failed to use it more often than not. That Sioux and I were sitting there all the while waiting, and the wind rising outside, and time passing by.

Then we stood up, shaking hands with the Colonel, and went out on the streets of the agency where soldiers and Indians were passing each other in the early morning, and farmers in from the countryside were riding up with wagons full of barter, and the wind rising stronger in the woods all the while.

By the time we'd drawn all our supplies from Quartermaster stores, it was past nine o'clock, and what with that list of gifts the Colonel had written out, weighting down two extra pack horses and two travois besides, I knew we weren't going to make any records for speed. But if the weather stayed good, it wouldn't matter.

We rode off into the woodland with the Sioux in front and me in the rear, the pack horses in between, and the sun bright over our heads in the chill air. I could see the Indian's knife sticking out from his leather belt ahead, and I put my hand down for perhaps two seconds, feeling the 15 shot Winchester slung alongside the saddle. I knew he was a scout, and the Colonel swore on his word, and I knew his father was a leader of the Teton-Sioux, but just the same I kept my eyes wide open, watching every move he made.

Damn Injuns

"Stop here," the Indian said that afternoon, reigning up his horse. "They not see us…"

He was pointing to a rise a mile ahead. We could see several mounted figures approaching.

"Why shouldn't they see us…?"

"All the same, better we stop. Wait here."

"But why, why? Goddammit, we haven't made good time as it is, and with the afternoon wiled away…"

But he had dismounted, was standing quietly by his horse, shading his eyes. I decided to let it go. I had authority to give him orders, of course, but everything depended on what he might be able to say to the old Chief; if we were to do any good, we had better not start in at cross swords. Just the same, I moved away from him by a few feet, took my rifle out. I didn't trust him anymore than I had this morning, and especially as soon as I could recognize who those four riders were: Indians, with Sioux markings, but coming from the southwest! Which meant they must've been off the reservation, hunting, because we were riding right then right along the boundary line. A clear case of infraction of the law, and I saw more clearly as they grew large in field glasses, the evidence: two large bull elks strapped across the horses of the two leading riders.

They saw us too. But instead of avoiding us they came riding right over, shooting off their rifles in greeting. It was flagrant as hell. After all, they knew I was a U.S. Army Officer, both of us were dressed in khaki, and they knew that game they were carrying couldn't've come from the land hereabouts.

Still here they came up, making the greeting sign, and got off, squatting down to have a gab. I was mad. I told Running Bear to ask them about that game, and he gave me a look and started talking with them. Then he said, "Plenty Indians go north to hold big meeting near White River. Shoshone too. They say Messiah is Shoshone Indian, not Sioux."

"There isn't any Messiah," I told him. "Ask them about that game!"

"They say young men from Brules band come many sleeps through lodges, crying out names against Government agency. Some go up to White River, hear Messiah make big meeting."

"What about them? Where do they come from, what band?"

After some more Lakota dialogue:

"Come from lodges near Laramie Creek. All friendly lodges. Not many from there go to hear Messiah.

"Laramie Creek's a good seventy miles away in the other direction. They've been off the reservation, hunting elk. That makes them lawbreakers twice over. I want you to ask them about that game..."

All I could do was write down the names, and maybe later the field agent would be able to take action. But this was a good example of how irresponsible they were. Order them to stay in one place and sure, they'd agree, but when you went up there to check up they'd be gone, not telling exactly where. Not that it was exactly planned, but these bands were always nomadic by nature, and even though the reservation was plenty large, they had to keep wandering off it, law or no law. One reason for trouble with ranchers in neighboring counties was this very thing, happening over and over.

But Running Bear hadn't said anything, and when I asked him again to find out about the Elk, he shrugged, gave me a peculiar look. One of the truants, though, finally began speaking, half in sign tongue, and half in English.

"All the same, everywhere on reservation, Indians much hungry now. Last summer plenty bands have white man fever sickness. Government say plant, but many too sick for working with hands. Crops very bad this summer. Also one steer for 17 days for one family, is that like happy agent words? Agents say no move, no hunt, be like white man. What white man watch his children die? No one come from far off to tell white man, no more do all things your fathers do, live on one land, never moving... I have spoken..."

And with that, contemptuously, he reigned up, rode off to the East, the Elk swinging across his saddle, the other three following him. They didn't look back once.

Running Bear's voice sounded exasperated.

"Light still bright. We go further now I think."

"Listen," I told him. "There's a reason for the Government order. Suppose every band took it in its mind to go off anytime it wanted?"

"We go further now?"

"Sure, and what's to stop any Indian from posing the noble native, just to excuse his law breaking?"

"All the same, we have good elk, supper time near. Now no elk. We go further…"

"Goddammit…"

But I stopped myself. Why try to explain anything to him? Only a few hours out, and homesteaders' lives hanging on what we might be able to do, and what was the point of trying to hammer common sense into that thick Lakota skull, but later that day we passed near the Woolf place, a rancher living near the Southwest boundary line, and found Woolf sitting on his horse near the corral, his rifle cocked, his hands strung alongside, armed.

"No offense," he said. "But we have to make sure whose horses are coming. I packed my wife and daughter back to Rushville for a while, too. The way those damn injuns are running around…"

"Why," I asked him. "Was there anything definite?"

"Definite!" Woolf said, and laughed. "Last night in the middle of the damn night, here come these four Sioux pounding on the door, and I asked them what they wanted, and they said water, and I said for them to put their rifles down, and I'd give it to them, and they wouldn't, and I wouldn't neither. You think I want to be slaughtered like Moran was on Angler's Creek? Well, the next thing I knew they began muttering at me and came riding over to the corral, aiming to steal a horse or two for good measure. We began shooting at 'em so they run off, but I ain't taking any chances. Damn injuns: The Army ought to teach 'em a lesson, burn out a few dozen hogans somewhere…."

I looked at Running Bear. He just sat there, impassive on his horse, saying nothing. What I wanted was for him to get that damn superior expression off his face, eat crow for once. Because his 'noble' chums weren't anything more than horse thieves plain and simple, or maybe even worse. And all the time I'd been getting ready to have some doubts, entertaining silly second thoughts about how all this ugliness might have been avoided, if enough character on both sides could be found.

All through supper I kept getting angrier, seeing myself as six different kinds of fool, and the cold beans Wolf fed us placed against the image of those dead elk, roasted and coal blackened from the fire, didn't help any either.

Later on, all of us took our turn standing guard at Woolf's corral. But not Running Bear. Woolf said a uniform didn't make a man over, and as far as he was concerned, an Indian was an Indian, and he wasn't leaving one to guard against others.

That night we all slept in the ranch house. But the Sioux refused to come in, camped out in his blankets near Woolf's pasturage. And squatting there in an improvised hogan strung between trees, turbaned in blankest over khaki, his pipe making a glow in that jet black, he looked less and less like an employee of the military, more and more like a blanket Indian again, reverting back to type on the reservation.

And all the time I stood guard, I could feel his eyes on me, watching me.

With only a Knife

About the middle of the next morning, after we'd made four good miles, the wind suddenly came up, cold and icy from the North.

We reigned up and stood watching. It was marvelous the way you could see the rain squall approaching, rushing down from the highland ahead like a moving milky cloud, proceeded by that vicious cold air. Where we were, out on the open plain halfway between Arrow Butte and Yellow Creek, we were caught with only our covering to keep us protected. Still I thought if we made a run for it, we might reach the shelter of the woodland several miles to the Northeast, brace ourselves behind the shaking trees.

But Running Bear thought differently.

"Rain and wind come here maybe ten, fifteen minutes. We be stopped in storm. Not pull travois, maybe lose all supplies on travois and trail too. But I know better way. You follow quick over this plain now, yes?"

"No," I told him. "I want to keep straight ahead. And if you're thinking of any side excursions..."

"Not much time make talk like this. We go now?"

"We're going straight to the woodland on ahead," I told him. "Because I don't want to lose any more time. And this way..."

"Not make woodland now. Maybe lose travois too. You follow?"

My answer was to kick my spurs, trot the pinto off into the direction of the wind which was fierce by now, dove deep into your lungs like something cold and fiery at the same time, and my whole face was becoming numb.

Then I saw the Indian wasn't with me; he was rushing off to the southeast, taking the travois with him full of leather goods and tobacco, and everything else the Colonel had made us pack. Trying to steal the whole damn business! I shouted at him to pull up, and when nothing happened I pulled the rifle out and fired one shot over his head.

The bullet startled the big gray bringing up the rear travois. Like in a nightmare I saw the horse buckle up, rear and bolt, dragging that rickety travois behind, spraying bundles off as he ran, the wind and hail all around now, and both of us chasing after. It was a near thing. If that horse hadn't decided to run against the wind, we mightn't have caught him. But Running Bear reached him first, grabbing the bridle, pulling him around and without losing a second, dashing straight over to the plain to the Southeast, myself following behind. By now it was clear, he'd been right all along. If we'd gone on, the storm would've let loose on us before we got halfway to the woods, and then we might've lost everything, travois, horses, maps, and the whole business.

But where were we heading for? There I was, carrying the authority of the military, blindly following after that blanket Indian, and the butte rushing past, and the reservation full of crazed-up Sioux all around us.

But Running Bear never looked back once, just took it for granted I'd follow, leading across the flat land and down a little rise, and all at once he'd come into a kind of miniature canyon and dismounted, disappearing around a corner. I got there in time to see him entering what looked like a mammoth cave, big enough for horses to enter too, though the big gray whinnied and shied back, and there was a bad moment or two when I thought he was going to bolt again.

Bad moment? It wasn't anything to what we lived through the next ten minutes!

I was shaking the rain off, getting ready to make some kind of fire in the pitch black, and Running Bear had gone out to drag in that lead travois, and the horses were whinnying and neighing with fright, when all at once one of them gave a regular scream, and the same instant another sound roared up in the cavern. From way back in the pitch blackness of the narrowing rock a shape loomed up, moving with awful clumsy speed and animal ferocity. I barely got out of the way of the first lunge. At the same time I knew what it was, and I also knew that my rifle was lying fifteen useless feet away on the other side of the cave, strapped to a saddle horn, and that against that awakened bear my hands were of no goddamn use at all.

Luckily, I didn't have much time to think about it.

The bear turned in the coal blackness, coming for me, I yelled, and as Running Bear, entering from the rain swirled mouth where the light was obscured by the storm, saw me trapped against the rock wall, cut off form escape by the advancing bulk of the maddened animal, he leaped across the open space, shouting something in Lakota, burying the knife in the animal's shoulder.

Afterwards, when I tried to recall the sequence of the following bloody few minutes, I found I couldn't isolate what happened clearly. I know that that crazy Sioux went for the bear with only a hunting knife, and when the bear roared with pain, the sound almost split my ears. I know too that somehow in the pitch black I managed to reach the tethered horse and my Winchester, firing blindly at the struggle going on where I saw the great bulk thrashing. Again and again I fired, using up all fifteen shots, and by that time the horses were almost crazed with fear, and the bear was on the ground, smeared with his own gore, and so was the Indian, though as soon as I made a light I saw he was crouched there out of the way, more shaken up than hurt. All he had was a gash on his shoulder which the bears' claws had made, and why he hadn't been crushed and killed outright neither one of us were able later to figure out.

For a long while we sat there, trembling in the dark and bathing our wounds from a canteen. Once I had to go out and empty last night's beans all over the ground. But there's something more to be added: neither one of us could've got out of that cave erect if the other hadn't been there, and yet my own courage measured against his left a considerable balance in favor of the Indian. But it was him who was doing most of the thanking presently, coming up to me with a solemn grin, pressing my hand to forehead and chest in a sign of bond.

"Going after that bear with only a knife," I told him. "It's you who ought to be thanked more than...."

But he shook his head. Then began talking for the first time with any warmth, saying how he had led us to where the bear was hibernating, his responsibility, and because I had saved him we were brothers to one another, and his own hunting knife presented to me as a gift would be the kinship symbol. I didn't want to take it, but his manner didn't allow for refusal. Yet it was strange in a way; there I was, a comparative stranger to the Indian country, almost ready to turn into a characteristic Sioux vilified, but that one single incident in a cave started my whole eyesight changing. People are kind enough to talk about my work in later years with the various Sioux commissions, and in Washington, and it's true, I've managed to do a little worthwhile good, especially in helping compile the Lakota legends; but if someone were to ask where the whole thing really began, I'd probably have to answer in a deserted cave, listening to an Indian tell me the story of his name begetting, responding to the dignity the mane evoked in telling with a conscious sense of its paradox, a tiny part of his people's history…

How long we stayed there, making a fire, cutting up bear meat and roasting it while the rain swirled and roared and eventually died down outside, I don't know, but the next morning we were ready to start out again. From the cavern's entrance we could see across the butte we had crossed, patches of night frost already melting under the sunlight, this mixture of hot and cold advertising the finicky changeableness of autumn in the Northwest, sometimes bulging the swollen rivers until you were half convinced the seasons had been turned upside down.

We made good time that day and after four and a half hours of riding, came to Angle Creek where a group of the Ogallala band Sioux were encamped, friendly Indians whose elders were unusual in that they had en masse been converted to Presbyterianism the summer before. We rode down slowly to the hogan area, firing off our guns, having the children and old men come up to us in greeting, holding out their hands for presents.

But after talking with them a few seconds, Running Bear turned to me, startled.

"They say Messiah is here, in Ogallala camp! They say he is a white man!"

Blessed, Blessed

Talk about lunatics, this loony was the champion, hands down… a tall gaunt red bearded maniac, draped in some kind of a white sheet over a blanket, and squatted in the center of a tipi near the Ogallalas' horse corral, banging away on the ground, hitting two stones against each other and chanting to himself in some kind of gibberish. I don't know what he thought he was yelling in, but it wasn't English, and it wasn't any Indian tongue the Sioux around there knew.

When he saw us, he shut right up, turned away, wouldn't even look at us. I tried to get him to talk, offering him cigarettes. I wasn't sure about the Messiah business, but I knew that the big ruckus on the edge of the Bad Lands was supposed to've been stirred up partly by some Indian prophet, and this man was as white as I was. He was filthy though, and he stank. Many Feathers who owned the tipi talked to Running Bear about it and by this time about twelve or fifteen other Indians had come crowding in there, most of them curious and anxious to listen to Running Bear talking to the chief of the band.

It took a little while, but after some lengthy dialogues, we had the whole story. A few weeks ago, it seemed, some of the Sioux had come across this erstwhile savior, starved and wild, in rags, wandering around the nearby countryside. They had brought him in, given him food and blankets. But then as soon as he had a little strength, he began to rant, walking around with mutterings and shouts, telling them in English that he was the great Indian Messiah sent by the Lord of Hosts, and that they would be the chosen tribe, because they had been kind to him. I could see right away that the Indians didn't take him seriously, they treated him with a kind of amusement, and at the same time with a kind of awe (which I later learned was because the wild spirit was in him, making him ill, causing him to blaspheme so holy a thing as the Messiah.)

I wanted to search the man right away, but the Indians around were a little afraid to interfere, so I had to do it alone. I found some stale cigars on him, and a few ancient printed cards,

"Zacharriah M. Hopkins, Spiritualist."

Also in the lining of one shoe there was a label which told us everything we needed to know: County Hospital, Needlebrook, Nebraska. So it was clear- Hopkins had gotten out of detention across the state line, and somehow, God knows how, had managed to wander as far as the reservation ground, convinced that he was descending from on high, with holy writ for the Sioux alone to hear.

But what were we to do with him, all these miles from Chadron, and ourselves bound for White River, another hundred miles away?

I tried to talk to the man.

"Hopkins…"

At the sound of his name he looked up, startled.

"Blessed be my people, whom Thou hast sent me to lead from out of the everlasting pit…."

"Hopkins, listen to me!"

"O blessed, blessed. Thy will be done. Amen. An I shall perform Thy miracles, yea, even though they crucify me…"

"Hopkins!"

But it was no use. We couldn't get any word out of him, and we finally left to go to another lodge where they made Running Bear and myself squat before the huge Army-issue kettle, serving us the traditional boiled dog soup of hospitality (which Running Bear said was a sign of esteem and friendship.) I was hungry enough to eat anything then, so I didn't mind, as I thought. But one or two mouthfuls and I began to feel sick. All around the old men were ladling the mess out with great gusto, and I could see pieces of dog guts floating on the top. I was wondering how I was ever going to get out of it, when I happened to think of the presents we had strapped to pack horses, and I decided a little gift giving might be a good way for saving everybody's feelings.

I went out to where I had left the packhorses, and my God, there was a crowd of Indians grouped around, and each had taken what he decided he wanted without asking a by-your-leave of anyone. Blankets, pots, tobacco, they were grabbing it all, and I got mad, tried to make them put some of the stuff back. The next thing I knew there was a melee. Running Bear came running out of the feasting lodge.

"No, no. We give what they want. Later receive back many gifts. Better not keep back things here."

"Keep back! But goddammit, you know why we risked our necks dragging these packhorses across the plain. If the Colonel knew..."

"All the same, these Indians good friends to white men. Many dangers for them to stay here. All the time bands from Rosebud come, say go to Bad Lands."

"These presents have to do some good, and it won't do any good to arrive at White River with a load of things the people can make themselves. If you don't stop them..."

But something else stopped them; as it turned out we didn't have to say a word. Because at that moment two young Indians came galloping into camp, creating an uproar, shouting and gesticulating, and before I knew what had happened, Running Bear had taken me by the arm, shoved me back into Many Feather's lodge. Other Indians near bouts were taking our packhorses, hiding them with the horses in their own corral. At the same time, more came running from lodges with rifles in their hands. (I hadn't known so many owned Winchesters of their own, where they got them from I didn't know.))

"Shhhhh." Running Bear put his fingers on his lips. "Everyone be still now. Afterwards talk."

"Young men from Rosebud agency come this way, go to White River. Try to make many young men here leave reservation land. Go to hear Messiah at big ghost-dance..."

"But who, what chief is..."

"Not chief. These all young men. Only young men like to make war sound here."

I took my rifle in hand, stood near the flap of the tipi. But I didn't like it; I was a bonafide representative of the military, and what was I doing hiding like this in a hogan from a bunch of marauding Indians? Wasn't it the military who were supposed to be in control of all the reservation land?

"If the chiefs don't have authority over their young men…"

"No. This be different on White River ground. You see. My father not want war anymore."

"But wait a minute…"

He put one hand over my mouth and pointed with a finger. At the same time we saw from the northeast, a crowd of horsemen riding into camp. They were in a helluva hurry and carried rifles, and significantly, they didn't fire any guns off (the traditional Indian sign of friendship, a voluntary disarming.) Here they came, pounding up in great fury, as if they were running away from somewhere, pursued perhaps, and some of them were painted up with what I later learned was the regular Sioux war paint, red against black, an open act of defiance to authority, since daubing was expressly forbidden everywhere except on certain festival days of the year.

They had something else with them too: a whole crowd of Indian children, riding in a wagon, frightened and excited looking. And up front with hands tied behind, and ready to drop from exhaustion was an apparition which shocked even the Ogallalas.

A white woman!

I looked again to make sure. Yes, she was a white woman, young, redheaded, and terrified from the way she cringed. I saw that her hands were knotted in back, and there was terror all over her. I gripped my rifle. Running Bear held my arm.

"Wait. Wait…."

"Wait hell! Painting themselves is one thing, but kidnapping..."

"Too many men. Wait till we come by White River. My father will hear me..."

"It's two days ride to White River. Let go of me!"

But just then in the midst of the melee, with those young Rosebud braves talking furiously and the young Ogallalas sullenly holding their guns, not making a move to join them, and Running Bear whispering to me that the children were from the agency school at Cripple Creek, four miles out of Rosebud, and the young woman one of the agency teachers, taken along as hostage so that the Walk-With-Guns, the soldiers, wouldn't follow – just then up sprang Hopkins, the loony Messiah, and before we could stop him walked right out, trembling, to the wagon, preaching in a quavering voice, crying about heaven and hell and saviors and salvation.

Everyone just stopped and stared at him, and the white woman came to life with a shriek.

"Oh thank God, thank God! Please sir, whoever you are, please tell them to let me down. I don't care what else they do, just tell them to let me go. The Army'll be after them, tell them that. They've burned the school at Cripple Creek, and two children were hurt, and they've made me come all the way and..."

"Heaven and hell," Hopkins yelled. "I am the Resurrection and the Life!"

"Please sir, please tell them to let me down..."

"I will judge mercifully; God hath sent me to be merciful. But Heaven and Hell – my people, the choice is..."

He never finished. From one of the renegade wagons, suddenly a shot rang out, and poor loony Hopkins fell dead beside the wagon. Which was a signal for all hell to break loose. I shook Running Bear's arm off, and rushed out, firing my rifle at the wagon driver, and shouting my authority, but by now there was shooting going on all over the place; the painted Indians were riding hell bent for the brush, the Ogallalas were rushing for their own horses after I yelled at them to, and that wagon with the kids and the white school teacher was bumping away like mad in the fast clouding dusk all around.

We chased after them, with Running Bear riding beside me, but after a few minutes of confusion and yelling, I suddenly saw that I was galloping on alone. The Ogallalas had reigned in, were talking earnestly to Running Bear who called after me to come back under the trees.

"Not ride further," he began, interpreting for the friendlies. "Too many Indians near White River. All picketed there, watch out for who comes. These not want to ride further. Afterwards white men go away, they be alone. Bad Indian come from Bad Lands, kill them."

"But they have a white woman with them! You saw her! So come on, we're wasting time...."

"Better we go back; wait for morning. You come with me to Spotted Eagle land, speak with chiefs..."

"But they have a white woman......"

"Too dark now. By and by too many Indians, may be two thousand painted there. We go back now...."

"Listen, will you go on with me yourself?"

"In morning. Now much better we go back, wait till morning."

There wasn't a damn thing I could do about it; no one would go one with me, and at night, in that strange country, I would have probably got myself lost in an hour. But I had seen enough to think that our so-called mission was impossible. Look at the way those painted Indians were worked up! Defiant enough to break into an agency's school, and kidnap a white woman! And we were supposed to walk right into that huge encampment, arrest the prophet who started it all, bring the chiefs back? No, I didn't see how the Colonel could be right anymore. The only language the hostiles knew was bullets, and how could you negotiate with crazed up kidnapers and murderers? Or was Donaldson's way the only way to stop more killing and murdering, and this time with dozens of U.S. foot soldiers as victims?

I didn't know. But by the time we got back to the Ogallala encampment, I was dizzy with speculation. And as if we didn't have enough to think about, what should we discover? Boyer, the Pine Ridge agent, and a detachment of fat white police from Chadron, fuming all over the encampment, trying to search the tipis, and making a hell of a to-do over the fallen Hopkins, and yelling about the burned school and vengeance.

The friendly Ogallalas were behind me with their rifles, when I saw Boyer.

"A brazen insult to authority," the agent was trumpeting. "Look at those guns. Who murdered this white man, what was he doing here? I'm glad you're here Captain, you can help us search the tipis. The school at Rosebud is ashes, I won't rest until we search every lodge. I want that white woman teacher found. If they've harmed one single hair...."

"Hold on a minute," I said. "Call off your bloodhounds...."

"Start collecting their rifles, Sergeant......"

"Hold on," I said, and pointed my own Winchester at his Sergeant of police. "Leave these Indians alone..."

"Why you don't understand, Captain," Boyer said. "The school's been burned, and this is the nearest encampment. Look at those illegal rifles. I'm going to search the tipis..."

"You're going to do not a goddam thing," I yelled, and suddenly I went really furious, full of cold anger against Boyer and his niggardly strutting police guard of wasters, living on the fat of other people's poverty. "These Ogollalas are friendlies, and I can swear that because I was here when the painted renegades came into camp. You're not going to take their guns, regulations or no regulations. They refused to join the pilgrimage to the White River ghost-dances, and that means they risk attacks by just staying here. As for the white woman, she's been kidnapped north into the renegade country, and that's where myself and Running Bear are heading for first thing tomorrow morning."

Of course he backed out. Naturally he couldn't go that far with his few police, he said, it was too unfeasible. And besides, his duties called him back, he couldn't be away that long. But if there was anything he could do for us, anything at all....

I told him that he could do. In three words.

But my God, what would have happened if I hadn't been there? Suppose he had tried to disarm these friendlies, provoking more slaughter which the rumor-mongers could turn against the Sioux? And meanwhile the bellies of these Indian kids all shrunk from eating dog meat, a luxury at that....

Running Bear grinned when I shouted out all these things. Told me I was talking like an Indian....

Please, Miss, Put Gun Down

Next day when we started out again it was already warm, unseasonal, and I began worrying about thaws; woods and plains were alternating around us now, and the country was getting wilder. Once more the Colonel's judgment rose up in my mind for castigation. A man doesn't care risking his neck with anything like fair odds but here we were riding straight into a lathered up mess of ghost-dancing Sioux, flouting the authority of the Government. And the mission we had was not only to escape with our own skins, but to arrest that phony savior, bring back the chiefs for a peace making!

After what I had seen last night, I didn't think we had a Chinaman's chance. And may be the quickest way after all was to bring on the troops, chase the Indians out into the Bad Lands, starve'em into surrendering to proper authority. Sure, some settlers and soldiers were bound to get killed then, as well as

Indians, but hadn't they already struck the first blow, kidnaping a white woman, killing an escaped lunatic to boot?

But Running Bear still seemed confident. "We ride into place where band lives. My Father receive us. Very wise man."

"Wise? Leading the whole band to the edge of the reservation to hear a half-baked Messiah!"

"Many people put trust before in treaties, smoke with Government men. Every year treaties broken. People cry for Messiah to save them. Better they go now, lose spirit of anger in dancing."

"How about those painted braves last night?"

"They come from Rosebud, dog soldiers only, young men without tasks; they make trouble like all young men."

"I wouldn't swear that General Fleming'll fall for the Colonel's parley now, not after he's learned of the kidnapping. And if he sends an expedition out...."

"No. We talk with chiefs. My Father bring white woman back."

"But if General Fleming sends a few regiments..."

"No, no. No expedition. We talk with chiefs.."

But I know why he kept protesting; because if the Colonel's plan was overruled, and the General did decide to launch a force to disarm these ghost-dancers, we'd be deader'n a dead hog on slaughtering day.

We pushed on, bringing up the rear behind the pack horses, and at noon we stopped by a watering hole, refilled our canteens while Running Bear bathed that wound of his which didn't look too good at the moment. He kept saying it wasn't anything, but I didn't know what kind of treatment he'd be able to get on White River, and I put a fresh bandage on. A gash about three inches across it was, below his right shoulder blade where the bear's claw had struck. If it'd been only a few inches higher and to the left, his eye would've gone out for sure.

We rode all that afternoon in silence, guiding those pack horses through small ravines and stony abutments, and later in the afternoon we began to hear the distant sound of drumming. To the north and south we could see the sky already beginning to darken, and Running Bear said we'd better hurry because he didn't want to risk approaching those picketed lookouts at night; he wanted us to be recognized. If he was tired, he didn't show it at all though my own throat was dry again, and my back and legs ached from all that time in the saddle.

Then later, as the sun got redder and redder, we passed through unmistakable evidence of a recent furious party of riders and suddenly Running Bear reigned up, stopped, drew me back behind a large clump of trees.

"What is it, what's the matter?"

"Look! Close behind those trees. There...."

I looked. It was pretty dark now, and my ears weren't trained for wild country foraging, but the Indian went forward, telling me to wait. Pretty soon I heard a voice cry out, and it was female and in English and plenty scared.

"S-top. D-d-don't come closer. I'll sh-shoot"

"No danger, Miss."

"I'll sh-shoot. I swear...."

"No danger here. Miss, please put gun down."

"St-stay there. If you t-take one step more..."

"Captain Delaney. You come, please...."

I remember thinking with annoyance what is she yelling about and rushing forward, and at the same time a gun went off, and Running Bear moved into the brush, and came out unhurt, struggling with a redheaded white woman, the same one we had seen before. Only now she was clawing and biting and yelling, and with her rifle knocked aside on the ground, and that Sioux grinning, though he was trying to placate her at the same time.

"No scratch, Miss. Ow. Please, no danger. Please, you listen...."

"I swear, the Army'll kill all of you. Rotten savages! If you don't let me go...."

"Why you do that? I not hurt. Only take gun away...."

"I'll ....make......you...."

"Ow...No, please Miss.....Ow...."

It was really a comic scene; in spite of everything, the mystery of her being where she was alone, and the nearness of those drums now, and the jeopardy this all put us in, I had to burst out laughing. I leaned against a trunk, watching Running Bear trying to ward off that redhead, and I laughed and laughed. All the time she got madder and madder, using colorful language too. Honest to God, she looked so damn funny, even though her clothes were all torn, and her feet scratched and cut, and so pompous just the same, invoking the U.S. Army when the nearest post was miles away and her alone in Indian country.

Then finally Running Bear managed to cut loose from her, and grabbed up her rifle before she could. Whereupon she turned on me, crying how she was Miss Ann Rawlings, a bonafide Government employee, and how she had been hiding all night, escaped from wild savages, and if I was what I looked like, a U.S. Army officer, how come I didn't shoot the savage Indian before he killed us both?

"Alright, simmer down now Miss. You better take a drink of water."

"Aren't you going to do anything? That Indian standing there, and you not even making a move!"

"He's a U.S. military scout, Ma'am. Don't worry, you're in friendly hands. If you'll just drink a little of this...."

"I don't want a drink! What's the matter with you, don't you understand? They burned the school, they took the children and me along as hostage, only I escaped last night, they thought I was asleep, I managed to steal a gun and break away. But if we stand here, not even move anywhere…"

"It's all right," I told her. "We can't go anywhere right now with night coming on… We've been riding all day, our horses are worn, they'd catch us sure if they came looking for you back over the regular trail. Travelling cross country at night with worn horses in renegade territory? No, we'd better make camp and take turns guarding till daylight. Afterwards we can decide what…"

"I'm not going to stay here for those savages to kill me in cold blood!"

"Captain," Running Bear said, and it was the first time I had heard him say a word for quite a while. "We lose much time, go all the way back now. My Father not want blood of soldiers. Never harm this woman…"

"I don't know. After what's happened, I'm not so sure of these chiefs controlling their young men. If they're all boiled up with ghost-dancing, and painting themselves…"

"All the same, not harm this woman. My Father…"

"Well anyway, you said before you didn't want to ride into camp in the dark, and it's too dark now, so we better wait till morning to decide."

"Morning!" My God, that redhead almost jumped at me again, tattered as she was. "I've been hiding here all day, just so's I could move when it got dark, and if you think I'm going to stay…."

"It's the best thing to do Ma'am."

"It's your duty, Captain, to see that I get back to Chadron. And I'm a citizen, I can report it! So I- I order you to take me back to Chadron."

"No one's going to stop you from going anywhere you want, Ma'am, and here's your gun back and there's the northeast trail, and it's two days to the Ogallala encampment."

"I'm warning you Captain…"

I just turned my back on her. I knew she wouldn't go anywhere far, but by now she'd got me riled up anyway, with her ordering and airs and commands. She was one of the prettiest looking women you ever could picture, but even making allowance for her being frightened to death, it looked like too much school teacher was still bursting through. At the moment I didn't see how we could help being delayed another few days while we brought her back, and meanwhile those White River Indians working themselves up, their drums pounding out, louder and louder as the dance grew more frenzied.

Running Bear and myself just squatted down, waiting, huddled in blankets, and made a little fire under cover of a stone overhang. And pretty soon here she came back again around the bend of the trail where she'd disappeared on foot about fifteen minutes ago. But this time she didn't say a word. Just crept up near the fire, shivering in the cold, and took the can of hot tea the Indian gave her. Accepted a blanket we gave her too, and curled up, humble as you please. I wanted to laugh, but I kept my face away. In front of us, the fire burned low in the dark to a few coals.

Later, I remember rocking myself to keep awake, and wondering what in the name of glory would be the best thing for us to do, and feeling the pitch black descend, and hearing those damn drums echoing and echoing not far away, the woods murmurs all around, and above, hanging still in the sky, the frozen stars....

Then much later on, when it was my turn on guard again, I found myself thinking back to Market Street, in Philadelphia, Pennsylvania, looking at my new gold bars in the windows of the shops, and wondering where the Army would be apt to send me for my first post school assignment. I had hoped it would be anywhere but out west, the great fictitious American west everyone read about where nowadays the Indians were tame and lived on reservations and military life was apt to be dull and routine. Nothing can be more stupefying than routine barrack life, and what I wanted was to go south, near Mexico maybe, or if

I were lucky enough to get assigned aboard to an Attache's office, why that seemed like the best deal of all because…..

Suddenly, I woke with a start. Pale light was touching the tops of the hills to the west, and the fire was a scum of black ash. The scout and Miss Rawlings were both sleeping sound, turned in towards the abutment like possum, but my first feeling was guilt for having dozed off, and this soon gave way to apprehension, pure and simple. I felt the sense of a hostile presence. Something told me not to make a move, or grab for my rifle on the ground beside me.

Then I looked up. There staring at me in an angry circle, red and black masks peering out of blankets, rifles in their hands, and surrounding our whole camp site in stealthy silence, was a ring of perfectly still war-painted Sioux Indians.

II

. . . .

THE RANCHER

Messiah Very Pleased

Every time the autumn comes around, my right leg or what's left of it, really begins to throb and hurt like blazes. Other seasons, 'specially hot weather, makes it throb too, but for other reasons. Well that's the curse I've had to bear – half a leg that's worse than useless, ever since the Gros Ventres Sioux ambushed the wagon train I was leading back in '71 when I first homesteaded out into this part of the country, leaving me for dead with all those scalped women, and my own wife lying there murdered, and the blood draining out of both of us.....

Not that I ever forgot either. Some of these late coming jackasses think the Indians've changed these past years, what with the reservation boundaries, and the pretense of raising cattle, and all, but I know different. Treacherous blood seekers, that's all they ever will be, and I said it a million times, a dead one's the only one worth-while. But what gets me crazy is to see how the Government's wasting our good American dollars on these parasites, giving them all that acreage they're just squatting on, doing nothing with it, and people like myself with cattle hungry for fodder, and the Indians letting their own steer run loose, or butchering them plain and simple, soon's they're issued.

That's why I was glad to see the Army come out here in force recently. I thought they'd send the troops out, show the chicken hearted Indian Department the right way to deal with savages. But no, coddle them some more, don't do nothing to provoke 'em, that's all they keep telling us! Orders from Washington! Well, and what about the genuine Americans living around here, needing that wasted graze for our own cattle, and safety besides form the thieving marauders! Don't we rate any protection?

But I found a way of getting them off their squatting hogans. It'll rile the Army up too, kill a handful of birds at one throw. Because this wild Messiah craze came just at the right time, and sure, I know that Mr. Prophet up there with his white robes and incantations on White River is nothing more than a Shoshone faker with a few buttons loose in his head. But he's not so loose he don't know the value of the blankets and skins they're piling up beside him as offerings. So all I have to do is play along with it, coddle his crazy pretenses, give him a few steers now and then. It's perfect – on the one hands, he'll tell us where he's going to leave these gifts to the gods, and we can pick 'em up one night, ship 'em east, make a terrific turnover. A the same time, what with his visions of the Indians' promised land further west, in no time at all he'll have those Sioux leaving the reservation by the hundreds, pushing out to starve in the desert. And when that happens the Army'll have to act, they won't be able to deny the cold fact of wholesale insurrection. So that's when everything will pay off, because after the troops are finished chasing those foamed up bands, there'll be a hell of a lot less parasites to squat on the reservation, and maybe some of us'll be able to get legal access to some of that graze land which right now is going to criminal waste anyway. Christ Almighty, I'd like to see Pine Ridge cut right in half, and there's plenty of ranchers who agree with me.

Just the same I didn't like it this morning when those Shoshones came riding into my place. I told them several times it was too dangerous to come here. I don't mind giving them food and flour for his royal divinity up there on White River, so long's they pretend they stole it somewhere else, but I don't like to have them come riding here to get it. Anyone's liable to see them, this ranch is right along reservation land. So I had them come around behind the house, tried to get it over with soon as possible, using sign language and pidgeon English.

But one of them, an Indian named Black Deer, kept dickering with me to let them have a few horses, thrown in, as extra gravy.

"No," I told him. "You take salt, tobacco, and that's all. And don't come all the way down here again."

"Messiah very pleased to have horses," the scoundrel said. "Messiah be very pleased."

"I don't give a damn what the Messiah is pleased about," I said "Horses weren't in the agreement. And I don't want you hanging around here."

"All the same, Messiah very pleased see horses. Make good spirit for Mr. Bergman."

"No horses! And that's final!"

"Soon all tribes make big dance, go many sleeps to place of new buffalo. Need many horses for much riding…"

The thing was, I didn't know how much of this Messiah crap they believed themselves; sure, they were using me, and I was using them, and both my own men and themselves kept loaded rifles within reach. But they never talked about the great savior except with perfect seriousness. Well they were Indians after all, and one thing I've learned, you can never trust an Indian to show his true feelings from his face. Never.

Just the same, that was an important place of news they brought. Because if he was planning to finish up that ghost-dancing and try to move the whole horde out, things were farther along than I thought. I didn't want to lose all that collection of skins either. So I tried to make it plain what I wanted, and finally gave them six colts as a sop. I was careful to give 'em young ones though, without brands, and believe me, I was plenty glad when those Shoshone moved off toward the northwest again and we could put down our guns and relax.

A little while later we had another visitor. Distraught looking and breathless, because he'd come a long way, riding half the night from Prairie Center. It was Boyer, the Indian sub-agent from Rushville.

Snivelling Old Woman

"A white teacher," Boyer explained. "They kidnaped her from the school at Cripple Creek. And when we got there to the Ogallalas, we found a white man'd been shot too, I don't know who he was. Some old man who'd called himself a messiah…"

"Messiah? A white man?"

"It was only some escaped lunatic, we found the papers on him. But that's not what's worrying me. The whole situation's getting awful, Bergman. That Captain and scout were there, passing through on their peace mission to White River…"

"What peace mission?"

"Colonel Donaldson's idea. He's had the ear of General Fleming ever since the General returned from Washington, and they don't none of them tell me anything, they hate the Indian Department. Maybe it was them started the investigation of the census, I don't know. Ever since I've heard about it I've been sick with worrying…"

"A census investigation! You never told me anything about that!"

"I just learned about it in a letter yesterday. Something's backfired, maybe the Colonel's responsible. But I told you it was too risky, I said we shouldn't've done it, and now look what's going to happen!"

"Stop shouting, Boyer!"

"I shouldn't've done it, I shouldn't've listened to you. Oh I don't care, maybe I should confess the whole thing!"

"Get everyone in trouble? Don't be crazy, Boyer! And besides, it's one word against everyone else's."

"I don't care, I don't care!"

Snivelling old woman! I knew all along what kind of a man Boyer was, but he'd been plenty high last year when I told him to cut the census count, send in lower figures. Sure, that way he was getting praise from Washington for less appropriations, and we had a talking point ourselves in lobbying for the reservation land to be decreased. Boyer himself didn't mind receiving payoffs from interested parties either.

But we couldn't have him rushing off to the military with his facts and figures.

"Take it easy for a second, Boyer. If you'll listen to sense...."

"Sense! No, I'm not listening to anymore of your crazy sense! The army investigating me, people being killed, the Indians on the warpath, and don't think I don't know how they're being worked up either!"

I got up then. But I didn't show anything.

"What do you mean, worked up?"

"Nevermind, nevermind! Anyway, I'm not responsible for what's happening now, no I'm not! But I know what I'm going to tell them..."

"Hold on a minute, Boyer."
"No," he said, and jumped up, his face twitching. Then he began rushing for his horse.

"Boyer!"

But he'd turned, keeping his fingers near his holster. The next minute he'd jumped on his horse hitched outside. Frightened old woman! Well, I knew where he was going, so I called McClellan, had him help me up on Big Red. Then we got two other boys and started after him.

But we didn't chase after on the regular wagon trails; instead, we followed a cross country route, racing on past reservation ground around the slate hills and through the ravines near Ambler's Crossing, and when we got to Fir Creek, all we had to do was get down and wait for him.

Protection, Protection!

What a sensation coming into Rushville! People running out of doors and saloons, women locking windows, men shouting for their rifles. Pretty soon we had a crowd in the middle of the street, and I stopped still, with Boyer's body draped across the mane of the horse, and McClellan and the other boys on either side of me.

"It's the agent! Look!"

"Where'd you find him, Bergman?"

"He shouldn't've gone out alone these days on Indian land."

"What I want to know is how're we going to protect ourselves from two thousand crazed-up Indians?"

"A stockade. I said before we needed a stockade here. How many times have you heard me say it? Yes, why…"

"Friends," I said, and I had to yell because there was a crowd now, a real panic almost, and I wanted to make sure it lasted.

"I don't say Boyer was the best agent that ever came here, and I don't say everyone here saw eye to eye with him. But that don't give any filthy savage the rotten excuse to shoot an arrow into the man, on his official duties within reservation ground. Who controls this county anyway? How long are we going to wait and let the Indians commit atrocities, running amuck while decent white men have to huddle here, without proper protection from authorized Government troops?!"

They began yelling and roaring. I kept right on.

"What's Colonel Donaldson's excuse for sitting there at Pine Ridge, with over fifteen hundred soldiers garrisoned and hanging around while every day the Indians get more reckless, and now have up and killed an authorized United States Government Indian agent!?"

The yelling became a growl, ugly and low-pitched. They were on a fair way to turning into a mob.

"We want protection!"

"Violence is what they understand, violence! I said it before plenty of times. Bullets and troops!"

"What about our property, our livestock?"

"Off limits! From now on Rushville should be off limits to any Indian.."

"Kill the damn savages. Take the troops and turn the gatling guns on 'em!"

"Chase 'em into the Bad Lands! We demand protection!"

We marched on the headquarters of the military at Pine Ridge and stood there making a tumult in front of a line of bewildered sentries with drawn guns. From inside the post, other soldiers came running. Indian scouts were in there, too, some of them dressed in blankets. Filthy spies! I didn't trust a one of them...

Then the Colonel came out on the veranda and someone helped me down off my horse and I came and laid Boyer's body on the wooden steps, and faced Donaldson with the crowd behind me.

"We demand protection," I yelled. "If you won't give it to us, we'll send a delegation to Washington!"

"Hold on," the Colonel said, and examined the arrow I laid there. "Shoshone," he said and looked hard at me. I knew he despised Boyer and the feeling he had for me was mutual, but right now I had the crowd with me.

"What difference does it make who shot him," I yelled. "It was an Indian, and they're all together out there, Shoshone, Sioux, Araphoe, they ought to be all…"

"When was he shot?" the Colonel asked. The crowd was surly, maddened as much by Donaldson's deliberate manner as by anything else.

"If you won't order out troops, by God…"

"When was he shot?" the Colonel repeated and I told him and he looked thoughtful, stroking his chin, and then began speaking, more to the crowd than to me.

"Right now I have an Officer on his way to the White River encampment to try and get the Indians to peacefully submit to authority without more loss of life," the Colonel explained. "If we don't get positive word in a week, we'll march on the encampment. But the agent's death was caused, it appears to me, probably by a few renegade Shoshone, because there weren't any Sioux as far down as Bergman's place, we had military surveyors over there last month.

"Now what I'm asking for is civilized action on the part of everyone here, and the courage of trying to find out what the truth is. I'm not saying that Boyer's murder isn't an outrage, and the sheriff's office ought to investigate it right away. But I am saying plenty of provocation has been given the Indians, and blaming the whole tribe for a few murders isn't likely to help solve anything."

"Look!" I shouted, seeing that Donaldson was liable to convince too many people. "There they are. Look!"

Down the main street, and heaven sent as far as I was concerned, a defile of two blanket Indians was coming, skins wrapped in blankets, in from the interior for trading purposes. The crowd didn't wait. In a few seconds the Indians were surrounded, and we would've torn them to pieces, only Donaldson acted too quick. Ordered three platoons of troops with fixed bayonets to bull their way through the crowd, surround those two scared Sioux, face the population.

Then the Colonel spoke again, looking directly at me.

"Bergman," he said. "These are Sioux Indians and you know who they are and where they come from; they're traders from the post at Cripple Creek, and we're not going to have any mob violence in Rushville, murder or no murder, as long as I'm in command of the Pine Ridge garrison."

"Then by God, we'll get another officer here. We demand revenge for Boyer. And what about protection!"

"Mobbing innocent men is no guarantee of anything except more bloodshed," the Colonel yelled. "Now I'm ordering you to leave Pine Ridge until you cool off, Bergman, and I'm ordering you right away."

"You can't order me anywhere. You don't have civil authority!"

"I have it in case of riot and I declare this to be an emergency, within my powers. Now take your men and get out of here and cool off."

Those two Sioux cowering, those soldiers with bayonets drawn, all loyal to the goddamned Donaldson, and so what could I do? But I let him have a parting shot even though the crowd was dissolving by now.

"I'm going directly to Chadron, and I'm going to prefer charges against you, Colonel, for harboring fugitives, obstructing justice. General Fleming'll know what to do, even if you…"

"Go anywhere you please, Bergman! But get the hell out of here now! Pronto!"

If he didn't have the absolute loyalty of that garrison, things would've been different. But I didn't want to risk a bluff, not with those bayonets and muzzles and gatling guns around.

So I turned, rode off, after yelling over my shoulder.

"You're not going to be in command here very long, Colonel. I'm going to ride direct to General Fleming!"

Across the Reservation

I really intended to leave for Chadron soon's I got back home and provisioned up, but a bad piece of news was waiting for me there. White, Taylor, and a few other ranchers were gathered together on my place, their faces longer than the northern mountains.

"It's the last blizzard and thaw that did it," they told me. "Railroad's abutments washed out, from as far as the other side of Rosebud clear up to Rushville. They're transferring passenger service on stages. But as for freight either way…"

They didn't have to finish. What with last summer's drought and the shortage of fodder, we'd had to ship grain in from further east, and there just wasn't enough rail stock to meet the demand. The same thing went for traffic the other way too. But slaughtering centers in Omaha and Cheyenne and other points always ordered to butcher on schedule, and if we couldn't ship as per previous commitment, they had the right under the contract to cancel outright, get their meat somewhere else.

And me with all those head of fattened cattle on hand, and my feed bins way down, and a commitment for delivery in five days to Cheyenne…

I knew right away what had to be done. But I didn't tell those others; hell, it was risky enough just for myself, and for a few minutes I even forgot Boyer and Donaldson and the Citizens Committee at Rushville, all set to journey up to Chadron, and waiting on me to join them.

Then I remembered what had happened. And sent Oakley in with a note to the Committee, telling them to go on ahead and petition General Fleming without me, pleading urgent ranch business was keeping me away.

Then I got McClellan and a few other boys together.

"Boys, we're going to herd the whole shipment up through Cheyenne junction, starting tonight. I want everyone to get ready. Saddled up, and get the wagons greased. We'll have to go over ground, and I want everything ready."

"Over ground?" McClellan said. "But Mr. Bergman, that's two hundred miles...."

"The railroad's still working east of Cheyenne junction," I told him. "That way we'll be able to deliver on time, and maybe load up with undelivered grain that's just hanging around. It'll be bought up if we don't claim it, and we can't afford to wait...."

"But two hundred miles, and part of it in the divides..."

"One hundred miles, McClellan."

"One hundr......"

"We'll go straight across the reservation," I told him.

They just stood there, looking at me. They knew we'd been on the reservation before, in summer for grazing purposes, and from time to time for moving a bunch of steer to be bought or sold because it was quicker and in right weather, there was usually graze to be found. Illegal? Sure it was, but the damn Indians were wasting their own steer, weren't they? Besides, they had twice as much land as they needed anyway, and it wasn't as if they'd know how to do anything with it if we'd let it alone to begin with... But that's exactly what got me so riled, coddling them and coddling them, and now us genuine American citizens had to think twice about moving our own cattle on the soil of our own country!

But I knew what my men were thinking of right now. Cheyenne lay in a line straight northeast, and from where we were situated, that meant going cross-country right near the White River renegades, next to all that ghost-dance craziness.

"Across the reservation," McClellan repeated, and the other men looked at him.

"A bonus is in it for everyone if we make the connection in time," I said. "Hell, we've been on before, plenty of times. The legality isn't..."

"It isn't the legality we're worrying about, Mr. Bergman."

Then I saw I had to convince McClellan before the others'd fall into line. "You all know the hostiles are ready to move into the Bad Lands," I told him. "Mr. Prophet himself has 'em thinking north is the promised land. And what about General Fleming? Soon's he learns about what's happened, he's going to send the troops out, and we'll be protected anyway. Besides, Donaldson's garrison's going to have to march, and take my word for it, it's not going to be any peace march he'll be ordered to start out on."

McClellan looked at me and the others came grouped around. I talked some more, telling them no law was ever passed says Americans should let their cattle starve, and the reservation'd be partitioned out one of these days anyway, and all we were doing was anticipating a little. "Is it Indian savages, or white American citizens has the rights to this country," I asked.

McClellan looked at the others, and finally they all agreed, after making me promise a sworn bonus in cash, whether the connection was made in time or not. But I didn't mind. With luck and weather, we'd make it with plenty to spare. The only thinking the worried me was starting out right away before troops left Chadron and Rushville for the White River country. I didn't care about the Indians, but if some of those technical military bastards saw our cattle on the reservation, it'd complicate everything a helluva lot.

And there was another thing on my mind, though I didn't mention it then: Since we were going to be passing through the White River country, what better chance to collect a few skins from the pile that his royal prophet had been hauling in as offerings? Sure, we could take them right along, sell them on consignment at Cheyenne....

A promised land, that's what the South Dakota country could be if you used your brain and guts a little. And as soon as we took care of the Indian problem, and the reservation land was open free and legal as it should be, without risk of any more connivance—by God, it'd be the Promised Land for sure!

III

. . . .

INDIAN

<u>MY OWN PEOPLE</u>

I had never seen such a great assemblage! Not only my own people – Cheyenne from the north, Shoshone too, even Araphoe with tips of bleached elk hide. In the place of the great plain by the White River we entered with wonder. And they who escorted us, Fox Lodge braves, kept boasting to me on the way, though it caused fear in the face of the white woman, she with hair red as elk blood.

"Howah. More than three thousand lodges are gathered here"

"For three days we have been waiting for signs. And it is good fortune for us when the Messiah will tell."

"He is great, a maker of medicine….."

"But thou shouldst not have brought this white man. The woman is bad enough, but the man…"

"Or art thou beloved of white man's ways? Thou, with the costume of walk-with-guns…."

"Howah. Thy father will be pleased. But not for these others…."

I did not speak. I walked through the great cluster of lodges. Behind me, the captain whom I owed life to talked with head up. He is <u>owaneke waste,</u> a man of much virtue. His Lakota name will be Shoots Straight in Blackness. Without light he slew the bear. It is a great story to tell in council lodge. But I was afraid. At Chadron, I told the Colonel my father and other elders of the Sioux have wanted all bands to flourish in place. He it was who sent me to learn to read and write. "Our people must learn." Thus he spoke to me. Yet here I saw many others bands, a sound of great ugliness. And other chiefs far from our reservation.

And this white woman, she with red hair, how could I speak for her being here? And if the soldiers should come with guns of thunder on three wheels? I have a bad feeling.

Wanukim.

We come to the tipi of Spotted Eagle, a throng of young men came running. Then the captain talked to me, for she with red hair had fallen on the ground. All stared at her.

"Can't tell whether she's sick or just fainted, we have to get her inside somewhere. Is this your father's tipi? Take her inside, maybe she's chilled. Here, help me…"

We carried the woman inside. I saw my sister-in-law and female cousins, my mother was stirring the bowl over fire coals. When they saw me they covered their faces. Then my mother grave me soup.

"Thou shouldn't care for this woman." I told her.

"Why art come so, with a woman of hair like fire! A bad medicine. And thou with a white man also……"

"Feed her. And that thou art good to her."

But outside I found a crowd of young Indians, their faces were painted. They made angry voices, shouting. I recognized many, for some had come with threats into the village of Ogallalas when I first saw the white teacher from Crippled Creek.

"Ho. There he is! A white man's servant!"

"Give us the woman."

"She must not stay on this side. Nor the other either…"

"The Messiah has come to lift up our people. Wankan Tanka!"

"Death to white man's ways! The Messiah will lift us up!"

They had with them a chief, Black Pony, a man of much bile towards other than Indians. I did not yield. My friend took his gun out, making his eyes hard. I was afraid he would provoke them, not knowing the character of Black Pony.

"No, "I told him. "We must speak with my father and other chiefs in council."

"If they make another move…" the captain yelled. And planted himself in front of the tipi.

I ran. I ran quick to the grand lodge where my father was. And with him also were Moon Seeker, Bright Feather, and other chiefs I knew. I brought them to the tipi. There stood he as before, his gun out. But none of those braves had dared to fire against his uniform of walk-with-guns.

My father held up his hand. He was oldest, had helped command in great battles on Little Big Horn when Sitting Bull had routed the famous white chief. Not one of others in council had led against Custer in that time. This gave him much authority.

"Howah," he cried. "Welcome to my son." And bade me come with him to grand council lodge, the captain also. And Black Pony, other young men too, followed us to council tipi of the gathered tribes.

Inside, all sat and smoke. We young men sat near the end, the chiefs were in the center. And Black Pony spoke in angry words.

"Why has Running Bear come back with this white man soldier to our people? We want no enemies witnessing our dancing. From all over many bands come to the place of hope. They have known many false prophets. These, "and he signaled the group of braves painted with war colors…" rode hard from Rosebud. They risked much, for they freed our children from Crippled Creek."

"Howah. That was bad." It was Moon Seeker. "Many walk-with-guns will come."

"They will not come. For they took a white woman with them, she in the tipi of Spotted Eagle. They will not wish harm thus to come to her. And should we send our children to schools of white man, where they may waste of the lung sickness! How many have died last winter? And where the white women says, thou and thou may not speak in thy father's tongue! Neither may thou visit thy own people!"

Much silence followed hard upon. I saw the faces were heavy with thinking. Then I spoke. I made brave words, though in truth I was much frightened.

"My father told me, go to the place of white men. We must learn other ways, -- thus hast he instructed me. I went. I saw much. Fear was with me, I sang of valor, for my courage's sake. Then the soldier chief's taught me. They were good. And soon I saw how it was, that the old time must pass, for their power is greater, in many things their wisdom is beyond knowing. I told the Colonel Donaldson, he who speaks our tongue, let me ride to place of the great gathering. He sent me. He gave me another chief to ride all the way with me…"

At this point, they interrupted. The lodge was filled with shouting. Many looked with anger at Captain Delaney. Black Pony's voice filled the air with hatred.

"Send him away! We want no spying on the rites of this time......"

"Away! Or that he is destroyed..."

"No more talking. For the medicine will be badly wounded...."

"He will talk against us. No more, we will see them no more..."

Then my father held his hand up. They stopped. And I told about the bear, how the turned away the white men police, saying, "He hath been as my brother. And that he may be received here as friend. Kola."

I showed them my shoulder too, where the wound lay.

They watched. And finally my father, Spotted Eagle, rose to speak.

"My son speaks in council. I am satisfied to hear him. And of this white man also; he has taken soup together with Running Bear. Let him smoke with us. But not walk on the ground of the great gathering. For it is spoken that only to him of the plains shall the dreaming come. I have spoken..."

Then I rose. I dared to speak again.

"Many walk-with-guns will wait for reply from this place. They would treat with all chiefs. No one will be punished for painting themselves. Nor for dancing either, neither shall harm come to them, this they have promised. But only that thou shouldst put aside this falseness of them Messiah..."

Howah, a great commotion! Black Pony arose, as if to strike me. His young men shouted. Blasphemy and prayers, songs of hatred, these they shouted. Then my father rose from the council table, came to the center of the grand lodge. And when he came the young men parted, for his wisdom was old, they were sore afraid.

Thus spoke Spotted Eagle.

"When I was a boy, the Sioux owned the world. The sun rose and set in their land. They sent ten thousand horsemen to battle. Where are the warriors today? Who slew them? Where are our lands? Who owns them? Is it wrong for me to love my own? Wicked in me because my skin is red, because I am a Sioux, because I was born where my father lived, because I would die for my own people?

"Now I will speak to the captain. The captain is here, and my words will be for his chiefs as well .He has fought for my son. I am satisfied to speak to him.

"Not because the Messiah has come, this does not explain the gathering by White River. For when we first made treaties, we knew our old life was about the end; the game upon which we lived was disappearing; the whites were closing in all around; nothing remained for us but to study their ways.....

"The government promised us all the means necessary to make our living out of our land, to instruct us how to do it, and abundant food to support us until we had studied well. We looked forward to a day of independence with whites. For was not his government also ours?

"Men were sent to teach us, a beginning of great badness. For they thought we could not understand. They came from the Indian Department. We were counted wrongly and counted wrongly again. It was a time of going back, not of going forward. We did not get means to work our land. Our rations were reduced. For two weeks a family got not enough for one week. Then soon some said we were lazy and wanted to live on rations. That is false. How does any man of wisdom think so great a number could get to work at once unless teachers came, also the means? These never were given.

"Even our old small ponies were taken away, and larger ones promised. But few saw them. Our children were shut up in schools, many died. And all the while things were done to break up our customs, the treasures of all our people. Many great chiefs were ignored in place of lessor men, and bad agents treated with them. Thus things went from year to year. I ask the captain, where was the army? It could not speak for us, it could only watch, though we had much preferred it to teach us as before. And those who held us made much talk about our condition. Our condition was a great mystery. We tried to explain this great mystery but were treated as children. Soon more treaties were proposed. The last in spring of last year. And right after we were told: the ration will be reduced again.

"What did we eat when our food was gone? We killed our cattle. Some thought of fighting. But what would wives and children do if the men died? The agents who counted us told us we were wasting food. How could we waste what we had not? We were mocked by those who came to study us. We were desperate in the hunger of our children. Where was our hope then? Soon someone whispered, the Son of God will come. The people did not know whether this was true; they did not care. They prayed and wept for mercy from Him. Some said they had seen Him. They danced in agony, with hoping.

"Soon the white men called for soldiers. We prayed loud for life, and the white men were frightened. Many said the soldiers had come to kill us. We did not know. We came to the beginning of the badlands, here we made a great prayer ground. For we will not live like before, where is the glory in such living? If the Messiah will help us, we will listen to him. If the soldiers come to attack us, we will die like our fathers taught. And I will tell the captain to think on what I have said. I am pleased to speak to him, for my son has told us well of him. But of the great gathering places where the prophecies are made, let him keep distant from there. The vision must not be harmed; neither must it be mocked if it is to come to us.

"I have spoken..."

He sat. He touched the bowl of the pipe, all were impressed by his eloquence. But soon a great noise was heard without, young men came running by the council lodge. The captain came outside with me, though I told him to stay. For they had shouted out terrible things: the white woman had escaped from the tipi, had run onto the sacred ground of the gathering.

The Vision of Wankan Tanka

Such a noise of drumming! And great flares on four ends of the plain where stretched the ceremonial poles, in tribute to the four sacred winds. We saw a great pole forty hands high in the center. A great number of Indians. They were of various tribes, not Lakota alone. To the left was a hill where the Shoshone stood, a one taller than the others. He was dressed in white. He held up his hands high above his head; never did he move them.

I saw the white female with red hair. She was by herself at the bottom of the great pole. Dozens of men formed a circle around her, none dared to approach. For she had walked into the heart of the ground of invocation. They made a circle around her, dancing their hatred. The Messiah stood to the left, summoning a spirit of scourge where the white woman crouched. His spirit would kill any man who ventured there. So cried the young men wildly, creating great fearfulness.

The captain told me to come. I was afraid. I stood with my father in the line of chiefs. But the captain moved. He broke from my arm. He walked onto the plain of the dancers, causing them to fall away from his gaze. He walked straight to where the woman was. He took her back across the plain. Then there was a shout such as I have never heard, they came with great eagerness to do violence.

Then my father spoke out to the assembly. "The Messiah hath told us whence his power comes. It is his spirit who will chastise the white people, thus he has taught us. Let us wait to see his spirit rise up against the desecration of dancing. For they have walked upon sacred ground, so they shall be withered. Thus he hath preached, as we have heard, all our people…"

The captain stood with the woman who cried aloud. The Messiah stood high to the left and spoke. All were silent while he made a great chanting. Then he prophesied. He told of the game which would return. All the slaughtered buffalo would arise. The hooves of dead buffalo had only to be buried, for others to come up in their places. Our people will become strong, all the dead will return to us, neither would they die anymore. And of those who had first come to the Black Hills, driving the Indian like horses into white man corrals, these would perish. Beasts would appear where they had stood. And with these two who have desecrated the ground of the dancing, it was only necessary to put them a distance from the encampment. Soon they would die, as it had been revealed to him. But whosoever touched them or came close, even as a man firing upon game, so he too would perish from the contact. And Utes, Cheyenne, Shoshones, these also would come to renew themselves as the Lakota. Thus spoke the vision of the servant of the great prophet Wankan Tanka, whose children are all the tribes of the Indian nation, glory and power to them!

All moved away from the two whites after he had finished, my father also. He motioned his followers away. They were left alone. And without horses too, all had been taken by the young men of Black Pony into the horse corral. Neither was there any tipi for them. Then the captain called upon me, for she with red hair lay faint, a sickness was upon her.

But my father held my arm. "Nay. For we have heard it, how they are to die…"

"He is my brother. My life was upheld by him."

"Even so. For it hath been prophesied."

"I do not believe such a prophecy. Leave me my father…"

"But though art without senses. I am Spotted Eagle who has taught thee all thou knowest…"

"Even with that, I cannot leave them…"

"The Messiah hath prophesied…"

"I do not believe him, my father. For thou has much wisdom, but it is not wisdom to bring more ruin upon our people…"

I crossed the open space to where the captain was. He followed me, bearing the woman who made a sound of trembling. I brought them to a tipi near the edge of the encampment; all fled when we came near for the dire words had preceded us. I made a fire, gathering herbs for soup. I brought them into where she lay. I brought blankets of my own and sat down beside her. As one seen in dreaming she was, for all that she trembled. Her eyes were black...

Outside the captain sat with his rifle, and no one came near to where we were.

Then later I heard my name. I went. I saw my father, with Moon Seeker, approaching, they had brought the stones of their medicine. For Moon Seeker was a stone dreamer, one who can heal. Even then the drums of the wild dancing still rang out, the moon was half way across the sky.

I went to my father, who embraced me. Saying, "Even if thou art cursed. For thou art my son."

They went inside. They made medicine. The drumming from the ritual of the dancing rose. My heart beat loud, and I was afraid.

A Shameful Man

In the morning, people began coming to see where we were, and many of my father's people came, also men of other tribes. For in truth my father was a large chief among his people. Many stood with fear several paces away from our tipi. They stared, expecting death in front of them. Behold, we stood alive and called a greeting. This was a great wonder.

"Howah. And is it truly thee?"

"But the white woman is not there. Perhaps it has begun with her..."

"No, they are all well. It is great medicine..."

"Ho, Moon Seeker. And art thou as before?"

"See, they are not stricken. A great miracle to see..."

They came slowly forward. My father beckoned them. But beyond the circle of the band another shout came, more angry words. Black Pony and his followers from other bands.

"Nay. Do not approach to them, for the evil will come..."

"But they are not stricken. See how they are..."

"Where is the woman then? Ask them for the woman..."

"But the white soldier-chief is not stricken. Lo, he walks..."

"And with the woman? Ask them, where is she?"

"They will all be dealt with. For the Messiah hath foretold it."

My father did not answer. He went inside, together with the captain. She of the red hair was brought before their eyes, the captain held her wrapped in blankets, everyone was thunderstruck to see her.

Then my father answered Black Pony, saying:

"Now I will say, my brothers, a presence of Wankan Tanka cannot be together in two spirits. And we shall do well to ask him, whence, cometh this failure of the holy power for Him? For behold, if it is false, he hath dealt badly with us..."

"Thou wilt see! Thou wilt see!"

"Nay. For some men are followers of great promises, yet it is wisdom to discover the truth. Come, let us go together to the plain."

They were afraid. Most stood far off, waiting still for a sign. And my mother was sent for, she that had been my nourishment, and went into the white woman. She trembled, for she also was afraid. But my father comforted her.

Then we all talked together. And I made the captain's words known to them.

"If we could show all those others the Shoshone Indian is nothing but a liar, a fraud. But he's still got them scared…"

"He has a great power of speaking. He has fasted many days, yet his strength does not wane. It is something of wonder."

"You don't see him when he goes into his tipi. You don't know what he does in there…"

"All the same, he has a great mystery for many people here…"

"But you're all starving! Look around, there's not hardly food enough for one time a day…"

"Even so, the people comfort themselves with hope. For the prophesy tells of much food soon to come…"

"If there is a fight with the army, how will prophecies help you? But that's what we've come to prevent. Because it's not the Indian Department now but the Army that has asked us to bring a delegation to meet with them a hundred miles east on Yellow Creek. They'll give you food for everyone, from Army stocks. But if you don't come…"

My father thought long. Then he and the captain counseled together. I went to watch, inside the tipi, I took the spoon from my mother. The white woman looked at me, her eyes were afraid. I fed her. She was beautiful in my sight.

I sat by her when she slept…

When the captain came in, it was not pleasing to him. But he had come to call me, for the friends of my father were going together onto the plain where the great gathering was.

We came to the sacred place. High in cold sunlight the prayer pole stood, the people still dancing round, and some had been dancing for three days. On all sides, women and children watched. When we came up they parted from us in awe and fear. Then my father addressed the great throng, while dancers stopped and drummers held their hands. And even he that made prophecies, stood up, clothed still in white. And these were the words of my father:

"Behold, let everyone see. We are well. Where is his power to prophesy then? For he hath told us, all will be well with us, our enemies will be as beasts, neither shall their bullets be able to harm us. And whence cometh this great medicine?"

Behold, the Messiah moved! For the first time he descended from that high place, and came upon the plain. Hundreds fled from his presence, they were afraid. He marched to the great pole. He stood with arms upraised; in arrogance he waited.

No one fired upon him, they were afraid to. For he had pronounced how the sacred medicine would turn bullets around in their path, they would strike the attacker, killing thus all white enemies of the Indian nation. He scorned the guns around him, and they were silent. Hundreds shrank back from his spell.

Then the captain moved, and his rifle spoke once, loud. A great yell went up. Everyone saw the Shoshone fall on the ground by the sacred stake. He thrashed like a badger, screaming. It was not proud. The people mocked him. As a woman or a shameful man… so he cried aloud.

From all sides then, Utes, Cheyenne, Sioux, the people looked to the Spotted Eagle to instruct them. And when he spoke, his words were wise.

Terrible to See

Thus it happened that we started for a meeting with the soldier chiefs. Together with Bright Feather, and Calagaya, the Utes chiefs, the Sioux elders rode on the trail to the southeast. Young Indians on horses escorted them, two wagons rode in between.

I rode with Elk, a nephew of Moon Seeker, of the Teton Sioux. But my mind was troubled by the white woman. I wanted to look upon her again. As a child without will, so I was before the sight of her…

Instead, I went to the second wagon where the old chiefs sat. They were all dressed with glory. My father, Spotted Eagle, looked the finest, but his face was dark. He spoke sorrowful words of the hunger of the nation. And it had been promised in the speech of the captain that food would be given. Yet, the Indians remained on White River. And not until their own chiefs returned to them and begged them to come back, would they return without fear to the reservation ground.

The captain rode alone. He was my brother. Owanaye waste, a man of great virtue. He had been very brave. He did not speak to anyone now.

The Shoshone, he who made prophecies, lay ill in his tipi. His followers made great medicine for him, for thy believed yet in his word. My father hath said, leave the man, though the captain had asked to arrest him in the names of the soldier chiefs. But this was not right now. The Shoshone were proud, they had been much humiliated in the eyes of all the tribes. If the captain had tried to arrest a false prophet, there would be killing among the nation. These were the words my father spoke.

Later, we heard a great noise like a thunder of many hooves…

Behold, ahead on an open place, we saw a great herd moving. Some thought it was a miracle of buffaloes. They were afraid. Calagaya said that the Shoshone had been right, for spirit was sending food to the Indians, as it had been prophesied.

The chiefs descended, they said they would look. The captain went with them, also several young braves. I remained with the wagons. The woman came out to look. I had hoped for that.

Then we heard a firing of rifles. I listened. I thought our young men were hunting the herd, for food. I felt it was good. But the firing became large, I became afraid. I rode fast, leaving others with the wagons.

A terrible sight! My father was on the ground, also Moon Seeker. There was much confusion. White men were shooting at us, the Captain was shooting back. I saw some fall. The herd was wildly running, it was a white man's cattle herd. I saw a fat white man ride away to the east, chasing cattle. Then our young men began slaughtering the charging animals, the herd grew fearful, roaring in great panic. Soon they ran in great fury, everything fell beneath them.

I saw the Captain's horse in the way of stampede. He was trapped by many beasts rushing. I rode close. I pulled him from his horse. My head was singing with many thoughts. The Captain shouted:

"If they hadn't stampeded, we would've been able to catch him. Because this time we caught him flat guilty, Bergman and his men moving his herd on reservation ground. See, it's his brand.... But I tried to tell, to warn the Chiefs not to order their young men to kill the animals, even if it was illegal of Bergman, bringing his herd across Indian land. I knew they'd open fire right away... and when he rode across that open space all by himself to talk with them, he was a clay pigeon..... But don't worry, as soon as Colonel Donaldson hears..."

I didn't listen. I saw my father on the ground, his great feathers were soaked with blood. His eyes were closed. Moon Seeker lay still also, as did several others. It was terrible to look upon.

My heart raged. I saw how it was, that this land was no longer ours. The peacemaker could not prevail. My father had wanted a little food for his people, and not to chastise these white men for using land that in truth was his. But how would it be, from this moment on? A great talking, while the nation went hungry. Nor could I see hearts turning to us. And those who had killed Spotted Eagle would arrange their victory. It would be managed against us.

I ordered everyone to turn about. The Captain was shouting at me.

"No. We have to go on. If we keep the rendezvous, maybe they'll be able to swear out a warrant in time. Because how do we know that Bergman won't leave the county for a while? And anyway, you know what'll happen if no peace delegation shows up by Saturday. So if just you and I and the teacher could keep on…"

I turned my back. He had no horse, his rifle was gone in the trampling of cattle. He had to mount into the wagon. She of the fiery hair sat there, fear was on her.

But I did not want to look on them now. I rode back towards White River. I had no kind thoughts of white men.

In death my father came home to his people.

A Prophecy for the Nation

Black Pony and other chiefs stood off, as it was meet, but they sang sad songs. They told of the greatness of the dead chiefs. They danced in sorrow and out their hair.

The people listened, many tribes lamented. My sisters beat their breasts, their hair was cut in mourning. And mine also, for I had thrown off all clothes of the military.

We came to a flat space by the river, near where the ceremonial pole had stood. It was torn down now. The maker of prophecy was gone, for several of his young Shoshone men had taken him away; they feared the anger of Black Pony and other chiefs. But now his presence seemed very large. For had he not predicted much calamity?

Inside a tipi sat she of the red hair, my female relatives did not speak to her. The Captain also, he remained in another lodge. They were made to stay inside, young men guarded them. For we did not want to look upon their faces then.

And this was how it was that Spotted Eagle went to Wankan Tanka: glorious in all war raiment, wrapped in buffalo hide, placed on top of the burial scaffold made of hewn wood ten feet high, his horse slain at the bottom; together with his sacred stones, his pipe of peace, he went forth. His soul was borne up by the Spotted Eagle after whom he was named, carrying his spirit south to the place of unending peace.

Afterwards, I went alone to the great peak where the Shoshone had stood. I built a sweat lodge. There I stayed; a great pouring came from me. My fury fled.

Then I came to the flat space on the hillock. Four sticks I placed in the earth, for each of the four winds, and whence they come. From the east, the wind of the golden eagle, symbol of the sun whence life comes; from the west, wind of the black eagle, sunset harbinger; from the south where the spotted eagle carries souls to everlasting rest; and from north also, where the bald eagle lives, bringer of the snows.

Then I sat still. I made my spirit eager for receiving. Many sit thus, and to only a few the vision comes. I thought of peace, and sought a dreaming. The sun burned me where I sat, and no one came near to me. Food and drink I had none, nor of human concourse. The sky mocked me for no voice spoke, neither did I hear instruction from the holy places.

I waited still. Paleness grew in place of the sun, and I lighted my four sticks. With my whole spirit I sought a dreaming. I called to where my father was, that he might hear.

In neither dark nor light the dreaming came, and it was wondrous clear. Behold, I saw his face yet, though he lay on the plain. And his voice was greatly wise, though I had sung the burial song over silent lips that early day.

"By wotahe, the charm which thy mother gave thee, there is a prophecy for the nations. Thou shalt go far from white men, to the north where the land is promised. Buffalo shall be there, and streams, and the grass of the prairies, thick as on the hope of former days. Beyond the barren place, where no grass grows, there our children shall flourish as in olden times. Many songs shall be sung, and many lances in the hands of hunters, to celebrate the renewal of the nation. And thou shall tell this dreaming. And for thee is the task to lead.

"Howah. I have spoken."

I Speak Peace

The Captain looked at me with fury when I told him.

"If you take them into the Bad Lands, the army'll have to follow. And you know yourself what that means! It wasn't the army's fault if Berman…"

"No. My father speaks well. I am prophet for the people…"

"Listen, Running Bear, you worked for the army, you know the power of the army. It was the army sent us all this way to arrest the troublemaker posing as a phony Messiah. And now you're doing the same thing yourself…"

"No. Shoshone made false dreaming. He spoke war with white man. I take Lakota far away, no be blood any more. I speak peace for the nation."

"But there's no place for you to go, it's all craziness, a nightmare. You know how far the Bad Lands run. And without food and water…"

"Promised land for Lakota people. We go there. No make war anymore…"

"They'll come after you this time. When I tell the Colonel…"

"No. No tell. Later you become the Indian man, live with Lakota people…"

"Are you crazy! You'll be making yourself liable to more than insurrection charges! If Miss Rawlings and myself are forced…"

"All the same, you come with me, as brother to my house. And she with hair like blood, she also. As a woman of the Sioux nation…"

"No! You wouldn't dare do that! I'm telling you, when they find out…"

He shouted. He made as if to strike. But Black Pony's braves came fast. They took the paper from him, - the paper the Colonel had given, telling where to meet with soldiers. But if I did not act thus, he would meet too soon with those of U.S. uniforms. We need to go far away first, safe from following. For we seek only peace for the nation.

And she of the red hair, if I let her ride back...

I could not.

The twelve wise elders praised me for my dreaming. The criers went among the people. All were glad to hear – even Black Pony was satisfied. Except that we did not kill the whites. But I told him blood would be no more. For our ways must be ways of peace.

That night we were a people of many tasks; tipis were taken down, horses were fed, travois prepared, dances were held to the Spirit to guide us where it had been promised. On all sides, hundreds were moving; it made pageantry beautiful to see.

But I heard a great shout near my mother's tipi. I saw many young men running, they were of Black Pony's band. For he who had shouted at me, had run like deer through the place of many tipis; without a horse he had disappeared into the woodland near the huge river.

We searched. We could not find him. I ordered the nation to make much haste. Back in my mother's tipi, she with red hair looked on me with fear.

IV

....

THE COLONEL

A FEARFUL THING

I've never seen it to fail, there's nothing more epidemic than panic. And the whole countryside was restive now, new rumors springing up over-night, all of it worsened a good deal too by Bergman's grand-stand play with the dead agent, coming in here and trying to incite a riot like that.....

Well anyway, as soon as a Citizen's Committee left for Chadron, I knew I had to get my troops out of Rushville as fast as possible. Boyer's death wasn't something that General Fleming could afford to overlook, -not officially anyway, and with all that pressure building up on him, and his own headquarters full of Custer-revengers, it wasn't too much to expect him to order a forced march north, peace parley or not.

But one thing I wanted to check on first. I took that Shoshone arrow that the agent had been shot with, and gave it to my own scouts to check on. And sure enough, they verified what I'd felt all along: the arrow was a Shoshone all right, but the arrowhead was a clumsy point, made from limestone, and like no authentic Indian arrowhead that any brave had ever carved himself – at least not like any I'd seen.

I told the sheriff about it, and then I gave marching orders to the men. But I didn't dare take too many troops because feeling in the area against Indians was still ugly, and if there were any mob disorders, I didn't trust the local constabulary to keep control. Not that Rushville was worse than any other place, but ever since they'd extended the reservation line over the Nebraska border, and ever since the fear began rising in the settlers all around, with the memory of the old massacres to think about, why a lot of natural good sense in a lot of otherwise decent citizens had just been plain panicked out of them.

On the morning we were to leave, after we were already started out on the northwest trail, we ran into a group of cattlemen, mounted and grim looking, and they had the sheriff with them, and a bunch of citizens from other localities in the vicinity. But it was a long, thin rancher named Johnson who did the talking.

"Something to show you, Colonel," he said. All of them looking at me and no one else saying a word. I knew that I was a kind of mystery to local people, even though I'd been foraging around Indian country longer than most of them. Indian-lover was the mildest of plenty of epithets they'd call me. But then from their point of view they were perfectly right, -a man who'd spent so much time alone out with savages? In a pioneer community, orthodox behavior is still a virtue, and that's contrary to what a lot of theories say too.

But anyway, I consented to go with them, and took a company with me, ordering the rest of the men to wait right where they were. And when we finally got to Bergman's ranch, I saw what the trouble was.

It was razed, burnt to the ground! Not even one roof remained intact anywhere about the whole place. Corral, barn, silo, feed bins, even the pasturage had been set to flame, and there were long stretched of grizzled black, with here and there brown patches. But nothing moving was to be seen – no cattle no horses, none of the hands. And Bergman, himself, seemed to have vanished into thin air.

The ranchers looked at me; it was plain what was on their minds. Because most of them knew about Bergman's ruckus in Rushville the other day, and it didn't take any imagination to see where blame lay, in their own minds. I hadn't marched on the reservation, and here was another result of Indians' perfidy, and that made me guilty again, plain as day.

Or maybe it wasn't so plain

"Not that I'm denying it was Indians did this," I told them, "but then where's all the cattle stock? I don't know of any bands near here trained to herd a flock that large away, without losing a single one. And how come we can't see a single sign of a fire fight, or a single body, Indian or white?

"If they came in force," said Johnson, "they could've overwhelmed everybody, taken every last one away. I could see the flames last night from my place, but by the time we got here, all we found was this..."

I looked at him for a minute. Then I began to think out loud. Bergman had guards posted all around, didn't he? And you mean every one of them could've been hauled off in silence, and not a single sign of bloodshed anywhere?"

"Are you trying to maintain it wasn't the damned Injuns that done this?"

"No, I think that probably Indians razed this place all right, but who they were exactly, and where they came from, I don't know. As for the other, the cattle stealing, and the disappearance of all these men, there is more to it than just Indians. But I'm going into the reservation to find out for myself, and anyone wants to come along is welcome."

They looked at each other. Most of them were willing enough, but they couldn't leave their own places, just couldn't take the time. And I knew what else was on their minds: a shortage of feed, and the railroad still being repaired from back of Cheyenne Junction, and them with stock ordered and undelivered. I had sent a whole company to help the railroad crews, and I knew that General Fleming ordered troops from up at Chadron too. But there was no help for it, - this was the kind of risk you had to take if you were bent on raising cattle in the Dakota country, all this distance from the supply centers, and the kind of strain that went into it didn't make men act much like angels in the frontier towns.

I got back to the main complement of troops as soon as I could, and we finally started out, with three of the ranchers along, appointing themselves a kind of committee for observation purposes. We made good time too, though some of the ground wasn't exactly easy for horses to haul those supply wagons and gatlings over. I was heading straight for the designated coordinates above Yellow Creek a good two and a half days ride from Rushville. What I was praying for was good weather, though right now the sky was clear, and the wind steady, with no more than a hint of coming frost.

It was still beautiful country, plains, and greenery and small hills. A land that something could be made of, though it wasn't anything compared to the Black Hills which the Dakota had given up by treaty years ago. But then the Black Hills themselves meant more than land and game, with the gold and minerals that'd been found there. More than iron wills and armies would've been needed to keep out the flood of prospectors after the cry of gold went up, and in a way, it was the best thing for the Sioux to have gotten out of there.

Still, they should have made much more out of their own reservation land, and it was pride and fear on both sides that got in the way, pride and fear, and little enough understanding from any quarter. A sad story. Well maybe someday when I'm retired, I'll take a crack at setting some of it down. Because there's plenty of eyes still turned with ambition towards this reservation, and once you start giving things over to the politicians, nothing's apt to be left. I was always against the Army giving up the care of the Indians to the Indian Department. Scavenger department is a better word!...But then that's not entirely just either, because there were good men around in Washington too, Chavez, and Senator Vorhees, and others. Only too much temptation got spread around in too many directions, and who's to speak up for an Indian in a Congressional Hearing Room?

Well right then, it didn't do any good to speculate any more in that direction, and as we drew nearer to the wooded country, I began worrying all over again about Delaney, and the Indian scout with him. If everything had gone well, they should be waiting for us right now with the delegation of chiefs. The old chief, Running Bear's father, was a reasonable man, and I'd been fairly certain that he'd be amenable to a conference, yet the longer I rode, the more doubt I began to have. Even subtracting half from all the rumors of violence that had come in to us, the disquiet still stood out as the worst in several years. And whoever'd burned Bergman's place hadn't been afraid to challenge the authority of the Army, only those few miles from the post at Pine Ridge. That was the biggest single act of pillage so far.

I began to increase the pace as my own worry grew inside, and about three the next afternoon, when we weren't too far away from the rendezvous point, we came across a party of young Indians roasting steer meat over a fire. They jumped up when they saw us, and made the friendly greeting sign, and I recognized the mark of a band from much farther north. But what caught my eye and the eye of Johnson, one of the ranchers who'd come along, was the brand on a dried hide of steer that one of the braves had rolled by the fire.

"Look at that!" Johnson cried, and raised his rifle. But I held him off, questioning the Indians in dialect.

"Where did you get that?"

"White men herd, Spotted Buffalo (the name they called our cattle by). They make a great roaring far north. We came from our village to see. Many lay dead in the river. We ate them. Our people were hungry."

"And were there white men there?"

"We saw no white men. Many white man beasts ran with great roaring. They were sick, a spirit was in them. They ran on top of themselves and died. They floated on the river."

"What's all that?" Johnson was asking, his rifle restless in his hand.

"He says they found Bergman's cattle running amuck farther north. No white men were there..."

"He's a lying murderer, that's all! Here, turn your back, Colonel, and then officially you won't have to be seeing a thing. It'll only take me a second to sh...."

"Wait a minute."

"Please, Colonel, don't let these bastards get away..."

"No wait, I just remembered something. Because these Sioux are from the Gros Ventres Band, they've never been farther south than this, and it doesn't add up to me, them coming all the way to Pine Ridge and in force large enough to raze Bergman's ranch. But if Bergman had left before that happened, say two days ago, or three, and had traveled with his men toward Cheyenne Junction..."

"Towards Cheyenne?"

"The railroad's delayed all shipments, haven't they? And what if Bergman decided to move his stock across the reservation in a body, try to make the shipment anyway by connecting with the emergency spur up near Cheyenne Junction?"

"Across the reservation?? Without telling us!"

"Sure, that'd explain what we discovered back at his place, wouldn't it? But what happened later on to cause a stampede is still something we've got to find out..."

"By God, Colonel, if he tried to steal a march on everyone else by moving out across Indian land..."

"I'm not saying that for sure, Mister Johnson. But for the time being, we'll just take these boys into custody until we can check..."

And I ordered those Indians to hop into one of the supply wagons, took their rifles away. They were scared, looking at me with grim looks, chanting death songs under their breath. Sad commentary on the state of relations between Indians and whites — that the appearance of soldiers automatically caused these Sioux to chant their prayers, expecting to be slaughtered any minute as a matter of course. And if someone else had been in command: Sure, that's what might've happened more than likely. And the record would've read: Killed While Committing Hostile Acts. I'd seen it happen plenty of times throughout the Indian territories.

We moved on, passing two or three small encampments, all telling of the great ghost dance north on White River, and the great congregations of tribes and late that afternoon, we finally made the rendezvous on Yellow Creek.

No one was there...

No Delaney, no delegation, no chiefs, nothing but the woods, and the peaceful creek, and the ominous silence all around, and my fearful responsibility for what might have happened rising up in me all the time like a sickness.

We made camp for the day, and I posted scouts out with pickets. And about an hour later they reported a long column moving towards us from the northeast, from the direction of Rosebud. At that distance we couldn't tell who it was, but the file seemed too orderly to be Indians. And I had a sudden intuition that whoever had gone up to Chadron to plead with General Fleming had done too well of a job.

I was right. It was General Fleming himself, and several regiments of soldiers, some new recruits just arrived from Omaha. He had a volunteer company along too, deputized ranchers. By the look in their eyes I knew I'd have to talk fast to keep them from killing every Indian that came into their path, who so much as made a flicker of a suspicious move.

"Colonel Donaldson, sir," I saluted, riding up to the General's entourage. He just looked at me. Then he looked around at the encampment.

"Where's Delaney?"

"Why he hasn't arrived here yet, General. But I'm sure…"

"Sure? Kidnapping and murder going on, and I get telegrams from the War Department breathing down my neck, and you tell me you're sure!"

I didn't say anything. I knew the General was acting as much for the sake of the recruits, as from his convictions. I followed him into my own tent and closed the flap. Then I started talking.

"WE'RE ALL HUMAN BEINGS"

"It's not so much that escaped lunatic being shot," the General said when I had finished, "but all these other acts of vandalism have got Washington up in arms. Boyer's murder was the last straw, and what you tell me now about Bergman's ranch being razed'll only make them scream louder. Bloody or not, order has got to be restored Colonel Donaldson! The Army has got to establish its authority, once and for all…"

"There is no quarrel with that, sir. My only purpose in sending Delaney in the first place was to try and prevent…"

"And now with that school being broken into that way, -- have you got any word about that school teacher?"

"No sir. Not yet…"

"That's the real cause of all the publicity. The newspaper are making a hell of a thing about it. White woman dragged into reservation under the noses of the U.S. Army, and all that. But God damn it, it is a hell of a thing, Colonel!"

"Yes sir."

"We've got to find her, or what's left of her, and I don't care if some of your precious Sioux get blown up either. Is that clear? And especially with that special Congressional Delegation from Washington coming out…"

"Delegation, sir?"

"Oh there's been a hearing, and some Senator from Indiana, Vorhees was his name, and has been asking a lot of questions about the census and Indian conditions, and it seems there'll be an investigation, but I want the Army's position to be unassailable. I've wired for a clear directive. In the meantime…"

"A real investigation will be the best thing that ever happened here, General.

"Yes, but never mind that now, that's nothing to do with us. Because we have to bring that mob back on the reservation under military control, and try to save a few white lives for a change. I got word only this morning that an expedition under command of General Miles has set out from Fort Yates to march southwest to Standing Rock where there's another bunch of Indians worked up in a Messiah craze led by Sitting Bull. And if we don't bring the northern crowd in before that, there'll be a bloody battle shaping up, because both groups could amalgamate out in the Bad Lands."

"No one's going to bring those Sioux in at Standing Rock, General. They'll have to kill Sitting Bull first."

"Good riddance, and I hope they do! But in any case I want to bring our group in before they get there. Because there's twice as many up north, and not just our own Indians, they've been coming in from all the neighboring tribes. If they should get word that Sitting Bull's been killed…"

Then he fell silent. I was thinking of Delaney and Running Bear. I felt pretty sure by now that we weren't going to see them alive again, and the whole mess, and my part in it, was making me sick all over…

The next morning we started out early in a long line of march, stretching east and west for several miles, like beaters in a brush, so that we could comb all the renegade country as thoroughly as possible. The General had the east section and I had the west, with Indian scouts out in front. What I kept hoping was that whatever renegades we came across would turn up in my section, because all those deputized citizens committee hotheads were with the General, and once shooting began it'd be hell to stop, guilty party or not.

After about three hours of searching we didn't find anything, and the weather getting colder all the time, and my feelings sinking like the temperature, but this part of the reservation looked absolutely deserted; no Tetons, no Brules, all the small encampments that our map showed simply vanished away.

Then the signal came back from the scouts awe had out in the front to halt the line of advance, and keep silence all around. I dismounted and walked ahead on foot, and finally met Sparrow Hawk, the Chief of the Crow Indian Scout Company we had. After going a little ways with the Crows, the troops halted in defense positions, we came upon a queer sight.

There in the center of a clearing ahead was an Indian burial scaffold, Shoshone by the looks if it, and piled all around the bottom was a great bunch of hides, furs, several dead horses, all the paraphernalia of a chief. Complete to pipe, stones, and charms. Two huge turkey buzzards kept circling around the top where there was another great pile of offerings. Only those hideous birds never quite came to rest because there seemed to be more than one body placed high up there, and when we came close we could make out three forms lying cross-wise.

And two of them were still alive!

When we came nearer we could hear an incredible dialogue being shouted out by what sounded like two white men, stretched out there on the death platform ten feet high.

"Hiss at them, Bergman, hiss at them!"

"Help! Oh help, help! Somebody come help."

"Quit that! I told you, the best thing to do is hiss when they come close…"

"I'm going to confess to God, yes that's what I'm going to do Captain. Because God'll save us, He'll have to hear us!"

"Sssssss! Shhoooooooo! Go way! Sssssssss!"

"Oh help, help! I acknowledge it, I killed Boyer myself, and was paying the Shoshone to work the Indians up, and I don't care if you took all of my cattle, God, I don't care if I lose it all. But please, please help us, send somebody..."

"Bergman, God damn you, quit that yelling! Because if you keep on, they'll get used to it, and we won't be able to scare them away anymore when they swoop down..."

"Oh help us, help us! We're human beings, God, just two human beings! So please, please..."

"Look out! One of them's going to settle on your wooden leg. Try to move it a little..."

"I can't, I can't. Oh help, help..."

Crack! I hardly aimed at all, and one of the buzzards fell right out of the sky, flapping dead on top of the scaffold. I was trembling from excitement because it was Delaney himself lying up there, I wouldn't mistake that voice anywhere, and I could even make out the color of his uniform in all that pile of relics. I sent two of the scouts to clamber up the scaffold, but they were afraid at first, I had to go with them. And sure enough, there was Delaney, all tied to an Aspen; limb, head, foot, and in the middle this old Shoshone Chief, more dead than last winter, wrapped up in a white sheet. And on the other side: Bergman himself, his wooden leg splintered, and raving like a maniac to all of us about God, retribution, cattle, and Indians.

But Delaney made some sense out of it after he got some hot tea down.

"Right there's two of the reasons at least for a lot of recent trouble on the reservation," he said, motioning to Bergman who was squatting on the ground, munching a hardtack, the dead Shoshone still on the scaffold. Then he went on to tell me quickly what had happened at White River, and how he'd finally escaped when Running Bear had decided to lead the gathered tribes to the promise land beyond the reservation in the desolate country. Then how he's wandered around on foot afterwards and had come across Bergman by himself on his horse, talking wildly to himself and vainly searching for his stampeded cattle near the river line. "His own men had abandoned him, so I arrested him on the spot," said Delaney, "but all he kept talking about was his cattle, he had to find his cattle, so I had to pull his own gun on him, and we started back, following the river line. But then these Shoshones came across us, the same ones I had seen at the encampment, and they had Mister Messiah with them too, and he'd been dead for some time by the way he stank. I thought they were going to kill us on the spot, but instead they decided to do it slower, and let Mr. Prophet have his revenge, so they strapped us up there with him on the scaffold, and we must've been there for eight hours already, and if you don't think I'm glad to see U.S. uniforms, you're a mistaken man!"

"But you mean Bergman was paying the Shoshone to…"

"Not paying. Encouraging is a better word…"

"Is that right Bergman? …Bergman!"

But he didn't say a thing. Squatting there, gaunt, scraggly, and wild looking. And then looked up and in a cracked voice shouted out defiance.

"One man's word is all! You ain't got an inch of evidence. I ain't saying nothing until I see legal counsel!"

HIS OWN BRAND

When we finally reached the river line, and the rendezvous with the General's complement, we still hadn't seen a single new encampment, and neither had the scouts spread out to the east. All this part of the reservation was empty. Which confirmed Delaney's story all over again about the huge number of Indians at the Ghost Dance Encampment.

The General didn't even want to talk to Bergman, who now was in hand irons and traveling in a converted prison wagon. None of the ranchers we'd brought along, Johnson and the others, spoke a word to him either, and my feeling was they'd have saved the Government a lot of trial-expense if we had let them.

But the General was full of concern about the white teacher, Rawlings, whom the Indians had taken as hostage from the burned school at Cripple Creek.

"That's what's making the whole thing a picnic for the Eastern papers," he told Delaney. "And if she's been killed..."

"She's not been killed," Delaney said. "But I think we ought to go out after her right away."

"Colonel?" the General asked and looked at me.

"Well, the men have had a terrific forced march, sir. And it's not far to the Ghost Dance Encampment ground. They might still be there. I suggest sending out a scout party..."

"They're not there," Delaney said, and his voice began to get edgy. "They went into the Bad Lands long ago. Excuse me sir, but I don't think we can afford to wait. Because in Miss Rawling's condition..."

"But where was that crazy Indian planning to take them, Captain? It's over a hundred miles of craters and dried up river beds and crazy passes, and extinct volcanoes. And cold weather's coming on."

"I have an idea, sir. But anyway, we might be able to trace them by their encampment fires..."

"General," I put in. "I think the best plan would be to move the whole body northwest before nightfall, to where Delaney said the Ghost Dancing was, and then we can see for sure if they've actually left the reservation. And after that..."

"No!" Delaney jumped to his feet, his hands clenched. "That's no good, sir. Because Miss Rawlings' condition wasn't any too strong, and out there without adequate food…"

"Just the same, seems to me the Colonel's right, Captain. What could we do at night in that wilderness? And then they might've changed their minds, they might be coming back…"

"No, no! Excuse me, sir, you don't understand. Miss Rawlings is all alone, by herself, and…"

"But I thought you just told us she wasn't in any immediate danger, Captain…"

"I…That is…What I meant to say…"

But luckily, right then something saved Delaney from the embarrassment of trying to explain. One of my own Officers came running, and we heard a commotion, rushing out we found a babble of voices trying to explain at once. The Officer detailed to command the prison wagon had allowed Bergman and the three Indians to go down to the river to wash. Now down by the river's edge we saw a crowd pointing to about fifty feet away and there, upstream, balanced precariously on a slight barricade of logs which topped a crude Indian dam at the point where the water makes a small cataract, dropping thirty feet into a gorge, we saw Bergman with his hand irons flying loose from one wrist and his wooden leg stabbing dangerously about for balance, as he inched his way across the roaring rapids.

I shouted at him.

"Bergman…Bergman!"

But the cataract made too much noise, and now dozens had gathered on the bank to watch. Even if the fool made it, there was no place to go, and him on foot, and the desert on the other side, and night coming on. That rickety crossing was swaying and weaving, and another man's weight on it might've easily sent both men toppling into the gorge.

"Bergman…can you hear me? …We'll…have…to…shoot…if…you…don't…turn…around!"

I raised my rifle. Not that I actually intended to fire because he was swaying so he would've fallen in, and what I wanted was a live prisoner to be convicted in public trial, so that some of the reasons for the Indian trouble could be ventilated once and for all, for everyone to look at.

It turned out, we didn't have to move a finger. For as we looked, we saw a large ugly mass come rushing down the river, and there were hooves sticking out of it, and bloated stiff bellies. Around the bend it came, picking up speed and heading right for the crossing that Bergman was on.

He didn't have a chance. It hit him on his wooden leg, and he gave a weak yell, and plunged into the drop and churning water, and the mass of whatever-it-was going with him. A piece disengaged itself by the eddies and whirlpools. A little ways downstream we managed to hook it ashore and then we found out what it was.

A drowned steer. From one of the bunch that'd stampeded straight for the river a few days before. Bergman's own brand was still recognizable on the side.

<u>A REASONABLE MAN</u>

Next morning the sky was that peculiar pale which one associated with snow in this part of the country, and by the time we had got the whole caravan moving west along the river line, the first flakes began to fall.

It wasn't a pre-season flurry, wet and transitory, but a steady downfall with the kind of consistency that takes hold, and long before we reached the western boundary the look of the landscape was changed. The trail in front was hidden away, just as thoroughly as if water had washed it out, and we had to rely on maps to check our positions. I had Delaney with me, and the harder the snowfall, the more restless he began to get.

"Out there in her condition! My God, Colonel, and with that snow coming down…"

"In whose condition?"

"I'm talking about the school teacher, Miss Rawlings. It's terrible!"

"What's terrible? I thought you said…"

"We should've found a place to cross upstream here, not delay like this, going to the old encampment because there will be no one there, I'm sure of it, and in this weather out there all alone with those thousands of Indians…"

He didn't finish, just scowled away from me. It was clear that whatever was bothering him had more to it than a nominal interest in seeing justice done. I didn't bother to press him anymore. All I was thinking of then was the Bad Lands themselves. Something like one hundred and twenty miles long and almost fifty miles wide at the widest point, and in between; a trackless, cratered, uncharted wilderness of barren, bleak, cruel gorges, treacherous quicksand pits and burned out waste where nothing could exist at all.

Two thousand or more Indians out there, and we had about a thousand troops with us, unless God, luck, and everything else was with us. We were headed for the bloodiest meeting with Sioux since the terrible massacre on Little Big Horn fifteen years before.

At noon, General Fleming ordered a halt, and we took a look around. It was just as Delaney had described it. The hill to the left, the river, the great plain with the great deserted ceremonial pole pulled up and poking through the snow, and here and there a dropped knife or carved kettle dropped in the great evacuation. In front was a bridge built of hewn logs and ingeniously buttressed with piled stumps, upon which the exodus had trekked, going off in a demented search for a new Sinai out in the crazy desolation of the Bad Lands.

Flakes were coming down so fast now, we couldn't see anything. We pitched our camp, army tents rising up where all those elk hide tipis had been, not so long before. In his tent, the

General brought out his maps, though we had to light an oil lamp to ward off the gloom, even at midday.

"That damn desert," Delaney said. "May I make a suggestion, sir?"

"Throw out the strategy books," the General went on, heedless, brooding to himself. "With only this one complement, and all those Sioux Delaney says are out there, and probably picketed too? Christ, we could go round in circles for days, until all our provisions and water's run out, without catching sight of them."

"Excuse me, sir," Delaney said again, and the General looked at him. "If you want a suggestion, sir," he went on. "The Colonel and myself could take a company of Crows and maybe one additional company of soldiers, volunteers, and go out ourselves. I think we could establish contact with the pickets, and I think that Running Bear would come out to talk with us then, he doesn't want a running battle, all he talked about before peace. But if he saw all these troops coming, with artillery, I don't think we'd have much chance of avoiding an open fight."

"Come out to talk! But bloody mary, Captain, we're not here to negotiate! Our orders are to restore order and Government authority, these hostiles have got to be shown once and for all whose country this is!"

"But they're not on the warpath, sir. It was peace that Running Bear talked about most when…"

"Peace! You call that wanting peace, Captain? Leaving the reservation against orders and kidnapping a white woman, and holding those outlawed dances! Oh sure, I know some men like Bergman agitated them too, but that's not all of it, they've been restless and ornery themselves for a long time, and they've got to be shown! I told the Colonel before I had doubts about sending you off with that scout on a fool's errand, and now listen to you, you're defending the worst troublemaker of the whole lot!"

"Just the same, he's not the kind of renegade you're talking about, General."

I intervened then. I didn't want Delaney to aggravate the whole situation by bringing on an insubordination charge, and I could understand why the General sounded so belligerent. All this mess riled him up more by its untidiness as a military problem, than by the issue of renegades. Besides, he had the entire responsibility, his whole career could be changed as a result of what happened, and especially since so much publicity had been aroused. So no wonder his temper was frayed.

But he could still listen to a reasonable voice, and I began explaining to him, cautiously, how I thought what the Captain said had a lot of real merit, because if we could bring the Indians in without a battle, how much more of a coup it would be for him. And all we would need to try would be a few companies, he could stay where he was as our base camp, and we could signal with flare or a courier, whichever he wanted. It was all to accomplish the end of getting the Indians to submit to authority before the sight of all these armed troops scared them into fighting against us. With the snow, and everyone probably cold and hungry, it might be even easier to coax them in than we thought.

The General looked at us for a long time. Then he walked around in speculative circles in his tent, and poked his fingers around on the map, snorting once or twice. But as I said, he was a reasonable man.

So at ten p.m. that night, in the still falling snow, with two companies, and one gatling gun, and provisions for only a few days of searching, Delaney and myself crossed the White River, set out into the Bad Lands.

ALONE

"Look there," Delaney said, handing me the field glasses. The snow had stopped. An early sun was shining above the crystalline white around.

"Where?"

"On the right of the oasis," he said. "Look…"

I looked. For most of the night, we had gone steadily forward toward the flickering group of what looked like campfires shining out of the old Grass Basin Oasis, and as we came closer and closer, we recognized a great number of lights. But now the glare from sunlight rushing off snow blotted everything out, and the reflection hurled up at us from the snowy plain almost blinded us.

We were freezing cold too, and I gave the order to the men to pitch camp, warm themselves. I doubted with that glare that the Indians could see anything in this direction, but if they could, everything would happen that much quicker.

"You can't see into the oasis proper very well," Delaney said, "but look on the outside…"

"Where?"

"To the left. That silhouette. See?"

Then I saw what he meant. It was a group of probably Sioux lookouts, with picketed horses, silhouetted against the western approach to the oasis. Behind them was no evidence of movement all. Our maps all say that oasis was uninhabitable long ago, but that's where they must've gone, even though right now it was freezing and snowbound. If we'd really found them, it was sheer fools' luck, since all trails were rubbed out, we had simply picked an eastern section of the desert to explore first, at random, and now had stumbled upon what seemed by all signs to be the rebel tribes, squatted inside an abandoned oasis, guarded by their own military-like formation of lookouts.

"What's the plan, Colonel?"

"They'll fire first, if we try to bring even this small group of men up…"

"What if we go on alone?"

"We? What 'we'?"

"I mean you and me, Colonel…"

"All the way to the oasis? But wait a minute, yes, I understand what you mean. We could go on by ourselves to the plain, right before the lookouts, unarmed, and where they couldn't help seeing us. And that way they might understand that talk was our intention…"

"Unless you want to try and brazen it out, bring up the gun, and…"

"No, I'm afraid, even the sight of a hundred soldiers would be enough to set the whole thing off. But suppose they take it in their heads to fire on us anyway? Without a stitch of cover,…out there all alone, by ourselves…"

I looked at Delaney, and read the answer in his own expression. Then I gave orders to Lieutenant Williams, and Sparrow Hawk to keep us in sight in the glass, and set that one gun out where the plain would be under some firepower at least.

Then I looked at Delaney, hitched up my coat, and started moving.

We walked out alone across the snow.

V

· ·

The TEACHER

<u>NOT GO BACK</u>

When I applied for work with the Indian Service, they told me a lot of lies. Danger? Savages? All part of the dead past, nowadays the frontier was as tame as my own schoolroom back in Rockaway, Pennsylvania. Oh sure, the Indians had their peculiar customs still, and one had to be prepared for a certain amount of oddity...but it was nothing that should keep a young woman with spirit from venturing into pioneering country...And wasn't this something to challenge the imagination of a young teacher? Operation Americanization? Of course, one knew that the Indians weren't far removed from primeval wildness, and one couldn't expect huge progress right away. But what better way to put one's own sentimental urge to serve into effect? Children were the proverbial plastic, weren't they, no matter where they came from? And even if the adults were lost, the children still could be remolded in the American image. Besides, think of the increased salary, plus the travel bonus. And think of the appalling shortage of women out in the north-west country...

I fell for the whole line, bait, hook, and sinker. Of course, there were mitigating reasons, - like sticky business in Rockaway with my good grey unflagging suitor, Elmer Blount, the hardware salesman, appearing punctual and ineffective, Saturday after Saturday, and the grey routine of classes, and the lack of social opportunities there. Or perhaps more important, the lack of that casual body warmth the presence of a family might have given, since I had been orphanage-weaned and orphanage-toughened from as far back as I can remember...

But I can't blame it all on that. It wasn't just a running away from boredom. No, I had too many dreams about being a regular heroine a la Nellie Bly, Esquire. Sure, sign with the Indian Service, go out to the Reservation with a Government handbook of Dakota phrases, and the U.S. manual on citizenship, and high and breezy ideas about the manufacture of U.S. citizens in my sweet little white clapboard schoolhouse, with my pistol on my lap, and the U.S. Constitution on my desk.

How long did that last? Two days, two weeks? It wasn't long before I found out that one kind of boredom isn't solved by bringing in another. Nor that, as far as my ideas about the Dakota children were concerned, I'd been a victim of too much Government Literature. Sure it sounded fine on paper. But with a bunch of silent rebels in the classroom, and the way they kept running away, and the superintendent's ideas about beating them every time they used a Dakota word instead of English, and especially the scandal of the Health Service, -with so many kids dying of TB, and so little provision for adequate diagnosis,- I was ready to quit after a fortnight.

But that didn't mean I thought anything was wrong with the government's purpose. A wild group like the Sioux had to be brought forcefully into the current of our national life, otherwise the delaying process might last for years. And wasn't the logical place to start with the children themselves? So although it was painful enough, the weaning away operation, I approved of the list of Anglo-Saxon names which we gave the children to choose from, and the exclusion of the old Indian games, with their attached nostalgia, and all the other measures which lay behind the simple philosophy of the Department: Americanize the children, melt them into the pot, and the sooner it is done, the better. That way, the Indians will cease to be a liability on the government, and the whole Indian problem will be solved quickly, once and for all.

Oh simple, simple! If only it were! But that was before I began to realize how much distance there was to be bridged, and how complicated it really was, and why a whole crowd of near-sighted men wanted to will away by brutal action what they couldn't think through in their own minds, (or what it wasn't in their best interests to think through…)

I was scared for my life when those Indians attacked the schoolhouse that day, absolutely terrified. All I could do was scream and kick, and I even forgot that brand new hardware store pistol lying in the drawer where it's probably lying still. Nothing heroic either in the way I fainted when that murderous looking one, the one they call Black Pony, came up or began dragging me outside to the wagon. And then that nightmare ride afterwards, the trees rushing past and my hands bound so I couldn't save myself if we had an accident even. I expected to be killed any minute, and why not? Painted up the way they were, and those awful cries, and even the children singing war songs, and oh, that terrible melee in that Indian village where I first saw Running Bear himself and the captain…

I reverted right away. White-woman-lost-among-the-savages kind of thing. All information and facts about the Lakotas absolutely vanished out of my head. And that's why I was ready to shoot Running Bear when I came upon him and Delaney later on after slipping away at night from the Rosebud party. Because there I'd been hiding alone in the woods all day, and at that moment all Indians were alike to me, and if only I'd had a little more courage, I might have actually pulled the trigger…

As it turned out though, it was Running Bear more than anyone else who kept me alive later on. Because when they brought the three of us into that huge encampment, and I ran out half crazed with the fever onto that plain full of dancing Indians, all shouting at the top of their voices, I was nearer to being killed than I knew. The captain walked out and picked me up, but it was Running Bear himself who found an Indian hutment for us in that freezing cold, and even brought me soup with his own hands. His father too, the old chief, came and risked plague for all he knew by staying with us the whole night long, singing his songs, and clicking his stones of healing. And that night my fever broke. When I awoke the next day, I was ravenously hungry.

But I didn't trust them any the more for it. I remember after the old man was killed by the ranchers on the trek back, and the caravan turned about, heading back for the river, I reverted right away again, panic welling over me, my lips and legs chattering in unison.

It was Delaney told me what had actually happened. Sitting there in the wagon beside me, and with the dead body of Spotted Eagle lying in front. And all I could do was wail like an hysteric.

"But what are they turning around for, why don't we go ahead?"

"They want to bury the old chief first. And now is no time to argue with…"

"But what have I got to do with any of it! Why don't they let me go on!"

"Stop yelling," the captain said. He put his hand over my wrist so hard the veins stood out.

"Please, please. I don't care about Messiahs or reservations, or any of it, I just want to get back. You're from the army, please, can't you…."

"Don't worry," the captain said. He held my hand. "They have to get this burial out of the way first, but there's no danger. They'll come in all right…"

No danger! My God, I'll never forget it! A whole day they kept me inside that lodge where the women kept wailing and wailing, beating themselves, cutting their hair, and groveling in elaborate grief rituals. And meantime: no captain, no preparations to start back, no certainty of when I could begin at least to look upon civilized faces once more.

And then finally the flap parting, and Running Bear entering, thin, intense, pale from cold.

"Where's Delaney?" I asked him. "Are we starting back now?"

"Please," he said, motioning at the blankets. "You make blankets close all around. Be warm in lodge…"

"I want to see the captain right now," I yelled.

Running Bear just looked at me. Suddenly I felt a kind of presentiment that comes with dread that drains your strength completely.

"Where's Delaney, why isn't he here, are the soldiers coming?"

"Indians be given new country. My father's spirit speak strong in dreaming. Very soon all these lodges go to North Country. All the time have peace there."

"But where has Captain Delaney gone? I don't understand! When am I going to go back then, who's going to take me back to Chadron?"

"Not go back," Running Bear said.

He looked at me. His eyes were bright in the light of the fires.

Safe to Starve

Next day after it began to snow, the whole caravan stopped and a few of the women where I was immediately began to munch on that dried elk meat they carried in their pouches. But I couldn't eat then. I was sick enough from crying and swearing, and two times already I'd tried to run away. No use – those women caught me, and pulled me back to the wagon, cackling and laughing till I'd've killed them with my bare hands if I'd only had a little more strength.

Not that I could've run far, even if I'd wanted. Because the whole entourage, horses, wagons, children, had crossed that roaring river and descended down the cliff side, and we were out in what looked to me like a ghastly wilderness; as far as I could see – bare uninhabited waste, or craters, and low gashes where rivers had been and barren lumps of stone. Nothing that looked like a sign of life for miles and miles. But they kept on through the increasing snow, chanting and humming to themselves, the men up front, the women and children in the back.

After a while I discovered that as long as I stayed with one group of women, and didn't run around and create attention, I was largely ignored. No one came up to threaten me or anything like that, and as a matter of fact, the women in my wagon, Running Bear's mother and his sister and all that raft of young children, nieces and nephews, were always shoving detestable food in my direction, spoonfulls of execrable soup, or dried up filth of meat, or bitter leaves.

Eventually my hunger got the better of my distaste. I ate with eyes closed, and expected to vomit right way. But that's what happens when you're driven to it, - all that filth actually began to taste acceptable, and I ate my share, huddling in the wagon with the other women where some of the older ones squatted, sewing with elk teeth on buckskin, and others hand carving clumsy awls and lasts. All the while a certain rhythm or chant kept up, lulling in its sound, and though I was captive among a mass of Indians deluded into insurrection against the government, with God knows what ahead, and no possibility of saving myself alone, a terrific fatigue came over me, the result of no sleep and fear and fever fantasies. I slumped against the canvas side of that moving wagon, and finally I slept.

When I awoke it was late afternoon. Darkness was coming on, the moving caravan had stopped. Someone had thrown another blanket over me, but even so, the sensation of bitter cold was immediately raw and penetrating. I went out of the wagon and saw the strange panorama stretched out in back and ahead, and above the snow was still steadily falling down. To the left and right, there was only wilderness, barren and tomblike, and nothing visible on the horizon, no life at all. I left the wagon, and began walking in the snow a little, still safely swathed in my thick wrapping of blankets.

But I couldn't go ten steps without coming upon improvised tipis, women and old men hovering, chattering, round weak fires, and what disturbed me most of all was the sight of the children themselves. Here and there I could see some of the same youngsters we used to have in our schoolroom back on Cripple Creek, and now that they recognized me, a few came up to me, trembling in thin woolen blankets. Oh it was awful to see them, their faces were actually blue, they were holding scraps of dried bear or elk meat in their hands.

So many blankets on me, and some of them with hardly enough to cover themselves, moccasins the diameter of wafers on their frozen feet. I took a few of the blankets that had been thrown over me, gave them away, and there was a vocal scramble as those black haired children fought over them.

Then I began to get furious...

Where was this maniacal trek going to end? Out like this in storm-ravaged desert country, with nothing growing, hardly an opportunity to forage for food, and all these families steadily pushing on farther and farther away from help of any kind, and every hour taking them another stretch further into such awful desolation... what would happen to their children later on? One more day and it might be too late to turn back in any case before some kind of catastrophe happened, with the storm getting worse, and the wind flinging snowy bursts into everyone's face. Then suddenly I remembered Running Bear's calm eyes on me, his voice raving fantastically about his vision of a peaceful life for the nation, and I decided to risk pleading with him once more to turn back.

Indignation alone gave me the courage to parade up along the long line of stalled horses and wagons and squatted Indians, blinking against the wind and snow, and finally I came up to where the elders sat, passing the long pipe around. Running Bear was with them, and I recognized Black Pony too, the saber-faced dark Indian who had first abducted me from Cripple Creek school.

I walked right over to them, and Running Bear jumped up, startled.

"No. Please not come here…"

"You've got to listen to me. You're the only one who…"

"No, no. Not now. Go back to women's tipi…"

"But it's not only myself. If you'd take a look at your own children, how they're freezing and…"

"Not talk here. Go back…"

"Where do you expect to take them then? In this desert? And with nothing ahead but waste?"

"You go back now. Please. Go back…"

Then a terrific commotion broke out. The old men rose, the one called Black Pony rushed close to me, spat on the ground. An angry shouting trumpeted from him. Then Running Bear abruptly began dragging me off towards the rear of the encampment, while I scuffled and shouted, humiliation driving the fear out of me, and the women snickering as I was dragged past, and a scroll of taunting shivering children running after.

We came to the wagon and he shoved me inside, pinioning my arms while I yelled at him.

"Wait. Wait! The army'll kill all of you, and I hope they do, I hope they shoot up everyone! When Delaney tells them what's happened…"

And I went on, with more of the same. But I knew there must be a huge cackling crowd outside in the snow, and after a while I stopped, and he just stared at me, calm, a curious pity in his eyes.

"Many strange ways in Indian life, later on you learn them, become wise. Sioux people not like women where elders make council… Hold blankets close around, very cold now."

Then he leaned close, seemed to discover several blankets were missing from the ones he'd brought me before.

"Yes," I shouted. "Go outside if you want to see why! Because I gave them to the children, they're freezing and shivering, and you're to blame for it, it's at your head, all this craziness. If you'd only listen, if you'd only take a look around…"

All he did was smile. And told me giving was the highest act an Indian could do. So there I was, already learning the Lakota way!

When he left I stayed inside. No, I didn't want to face those grinning female faces in the snow, waiting to laugh and shout mockery. But one thing I'd learned; as long as he was there, as long as everyone believed in him, I was safe. Not even Black Pony and the other intransigents would dare to harm me.

But safe for what? To starve? Or to freeze to death out in this godforsaken desert?

I felt the wagon begin to move. The caravan was starting once more.

Pilgrims and Pity

Another day, another night. The long senseless pilgrimage kept moving on. To pass the time, I began to improvise footwear, because everyone's shoes were so thin, especially the young boys, and running around in buckskin sandals the way they were, they were apt to freeze with permanent results. So I took their slippers, put pieces of out blanket inside, insulating them a little against the awful wind which never ceased at all, kept howling down from the north, day and night, though the snow finally stopped at last, thank God.

Soon I'd developed a clientele. One told another, and after a time children kept running to our wagon, pointing to their moccasins, and motioning in sign language, or in English itself, for the famous 'fat shoes,' 'fat shoes'....

But the actual hours, days and nights, of the fantastic trek itself, were hazy. A few vivid details stand out.

I remember, for example, when Running Bear and five or six men came riding out of the snow at night, after searching for hours, and carrying, when they came back, armloads of frozen dead branches for firewood. They went from fire to fire, dropping pieces off here and there, until nothing was left for themselves at all, and they came back to squat with pipes huddled blankets, singing prayer chants, gazing at the sky.

And I remembered when the remains of the hoarded dried meat went and nothing was left for stewing in the great kettles but the butchered limbs of household dogs and horses...

And the fruitless hunts. When the young men went out into the wilderness ahead of the beaters, shouting, their rifles in their hands, looking hopefully for the buffalo they thought would reappear, as by magic. And how the wagons waited, the old men, the women with empty pots, the ragged bewildered faces of the children, until the hunters returned, dark with rage, their rifles unused...

And the pagan despairing dances... Danced on the silent snow to a spirit that goaded them with false promises... the naked bodies of the imprecators, frostbitten by wind and cold, dancing a furious self-sacrificial prayer of self-immolation, their raw flesh open to the storm...

Three times the great caravan changed direction, because of Running Bear's divinations, like a great blind animal in purgatory, groping for paradise itself. But each time, though we went deeper into the desert, nothing was changed, - nothing but the locals of suffering...

I remember how Running Bear came once and squatted down beside our family fire, talking to me in whispers while the other women moved respectfully off, telling me of his father, and the life of the Indians... but I didn't even protest. Because by now a great pity had so broken my own fear and anger down, that the dominant feeling I had was an excruciating pathos, called up by the constant image of those Bible-like wanderers, confidently expecting their own magic renewal in a storybook country of pure myth alone...

But Running Bear tried to instruct me, telling of the sacred Sioux number, four; explaining how there were four winds, four sacred directions, four days of mourning after death, four great disasters. And these were in order: the loss of a wife; the loss of a mother before the end of weaning; famine; and defeat in battle. Also, another of his favorite English words was *barbarism*. Everyone agreed the Indians were *barbaric*, he said, accenting the word. And why? Because they never beat their children, or locked men up for punishment? Because they never hoarded more than they needed of game and plants? Or because they celebrated generosity as the greatest virtue of all?

But I stopped him then. Everywhere now the suffering was so widespread, the signs of hunger so visible, that I thought perhaps if I appealed to his good sense this time, and not for my sake, but for the sake of the whole tribe's welfare, he might listen at last.

I told him how baseless the whole thing was. I told him that perhaps what he'd done would be enough to make people realize how desperate the Indians were. I said that if we turned back now, I was sure the Army wouldn't arrest him, or put anyone in prison, as he feared. I told him they'd be given food to eat, and as for myself, I would swear to the authorities that I had no grievance to declare.

I talked like that with my fists clenched. Staring and hoarse, squatted Indian fashion in an elk hide hogan, shouting from time to time above the screaming wind outside.

And I got nowhere. For even while I was pleading, the party of perpetual scouts who walked ahead of the caravan, searching for sings of redemption, came rushing back to cry that an oasis was up ahead, a place the Indians called grass basin, where there would be shelter until the wind died down and perhaps wild animals, themselves hiding from the storm. So nothing would do but that the tipis had to be taken down again right away, the travois loaded for the fifth remove in less than four days.

Within a half hour, we were pilgrims again.

Whoop, Whoop!

Dead trees. Hillocks where cactus once grew, now covered with frost. Rocks, stumps, and no sign of life, not even a spring. The wind rising again, and a milky-ness in the sky which told of more snow. And here were these childlike people, dancing a thanksgiving dance! As if this god forsaken sterile oasis was the answer to all prayers, though all it meant was exchanging one kind of wilderness for another.

I sat apart. I had taken to sewing steadily for the sake of keeping my sanity up. By now, I had a large group of children clustering around, many of them from Cripple Creek. And I had taken to telling them stories as well. I figured whatever could take both our minds off would be a godsend, and the time so heavy on everyone…

Food was the greatest hardship, - greater than cold and exposure and fatigue. All of us went foraging beyond the encampment ground. All we found were some shriveled roots, which the old woman put into pots. Some even began killing their wagon ponies. And I got so that I could watch that too, without flinching. But whoever decided to kill his horse always invited a group of adjacent families, and by the time the beast was butchered, there was often little left for the owner.

They ate the raw meat, without cooking it; firewood was too scarce. A few finally decided to break up their Army-issue wagons. These were distributed as far as the splinters would stretch among the gathered scores of freezing families.

Every so often young Indians, communal hunters, left the oasis on foot, carrying rifles and searching for anything they might find, bear, elk anything. And each time they came back half dead and empty-handed, and another horse had to be killed, so they could get strength to go out again.

Running Bear ordered a dance, as deliverance from suffering, and they carved a long pole out of petrified wood, and some old men stripped themselves to a loincloth, howling around that pole, hopefully watched by a semi-circle of shivering thronged Indians. I was too weak to stand out in the open too long. But I saw one of those crazed frozen Indians fall down dead from sheer exhaustion, and another took his place immediately. The desperate dancing never stopped.

Then a cry went up one day, morning or afternoon, I don't know which, but I began to hear a cry, *whoop, whoop*, and two young Indians came riding into the encampment from the edge of the oasis where they'd been posted as lookouts. My blood pounded when I learned what they were shouting.

Whoop meant soldiers! Two soldiers on foot all alone, and walking toward the edge of the oasis on the crust of that snow filled plain!

Pied Piper

If I hadn't been half crazed with hunger and cold, I never would've done it… oh sure, I know that a lot of silly things were written in the newspaper later on about my so-called courage, and how I saved so many children single-handed, but it was myself as much as the children I was thinking of, and I just couldn't invent any other way.

When Running Bear refused to let me go with him, even as far as the edge of the plain, I made up my mind. Because right then the Indians were preparing themselves for a battle, the young men painting themselves, putting on feathers, Black Pony and his followers chanting war songs. Running Bear announced he wanted peace, and if the soldiers left the tribe alone, there would be no bloodshed, and we would yet see the promised country for the Sioux. There was no arguing with him at all. He had decorated himself with feathers and paint, and together with a group of elders, and lack Pony as bodyguard, he left the encampment and rode out of the oasis.

I went back to the wagon where the usual crowd of children was waiting. I told them we were going to play a new kind of game, and I would have something good to give them soon, and all they had to do was follow me and keep quiet. So much confusion was going on, death chants, and battle preparations, that nobody noticed us at all, and we walked into the snowy woods by ourselves.

I didn't know where I was headed for. But I thought if only I were lucky, we'd come to the edge of the oasis before long, and then we could see where the soldiers were. And if we walked towards them, nobody would fire on a hungry group of children walking in a defenseless body out in the open towards shelter and warmth for themselves.

Pretty soon we came to the desert's edge. We saw a group of men, Indians and soldiers, squatting together, smoking in the middle of the great expanse of snow. We began boldly walking towards them.

Tell Them to Turn Around

The Captain looked at me, then back at the other officer who was with him, - that was Colonel Donaldson, as I later learned, - then back to me again. I don't know what he expected to see, and I must've looked like a wraith of some kind. But Running Bear, and the elders had risen in anger and clustered menacingly around us, and right then we were still outnumbered, because all I could see were those two officers, I had no idea where the main body of troops might be hidden.

Delaney finally found his tongue.

"No! By God, I don't believe it! All by herself like a goddamned pied piper! Walking across the snow like it was nothing at all!"

"Are you alright, Miss Rawlings?" the Colonel said.

"Starved and frozen to death," I tried to tell him, though my eyes were full of tears, I was trembling all over with relief. "But these children are only a small part of what's left back there, there's others so much worse off…"

"No!" and Running Bear stepped forward, his eyes glaring while Black Pony spat on the ground, and the other chiefs made a warning rumble.

"Food and furs are waiting for everyone," Delaney told the Indians. "But not until you give your word to us personally that the tribe'll return in peace and…"

"No!" and Running Bear spat into the snow. His eyes were painful to look at, he spoke in monotone. "Once on a day I told everything of my father's dreaming to this man. He was my brother, he wore my knife. Then he turned far away. He made bad talk against me. Come here, lead many soldiers to kill the Sioux people…"

"There's not going to be any killing, nothing like that; all we want is for you to come in in an orderly group, and recognize the Army's authority. Do you want to go on starving, and force…."

"These children are Sioux children. Why does she lead them here? They must come with us. And for her, I do not want to speak to her. I have no thoughts to look upon her now."

But then the Colonel started speaking to them in their own dialect, slowly and seriously. They watched him, graven-faced. I had taken a sip of something Delaney carried underneath his greatcoat – brandy I guess it was, - and now I leaned against him to steady himself.

When the Colonel finished, the Indians looked at one another.

"I told them the army had the whole area surrounded," Donaldson translated, "and there'd be plenty of food for them if they'd come in peaceably, and no one'd be taking their children away. It's not Running Bear who's holding back so much as the others, especially that fierce-looking one with the black feathers…"

Then the Colonel stopped. Because Black Pony and some of the other chiefs had started to herd the children back across the snow in the direction we had come, and instantly I found myself yelling: "Sop them, sir, please don't let them do it! Everyone's starving and freezing in there, tell them to turn around!"

Suddenly several things happened all at once. The Captain's pistol went off, shooting a flare up, and there was a hideous crack a few seconds later as a shell exploded in warning a few feet away from where we stood. The children panicked, running and crying, I felt myself dashed to the ground out of the line of possible fire by Delaney; and the group of Indian emissaries made a sudden bold dash back across the snow towards the oasis, some carrying children in their arms, some firing back at us over their shoulders, some holding their war feathers in their hands.

I was aware of the Colonel and the Captain yelling at each other as I got up, tried to calm the anxious cries of children left running about crazily in no man's land.

"What'd you shoot that flare off for! I told you that was only in case we were fired upon first! And the way those Indians've run off now, we probably have a hundred times less chance of bringing them in without bloodshed!"

"But I thought it was an emergency, sir. The way they were dragging those starving kids off, and…."

"A damn fool thing to do! I think I could've brought Running Bear around in time. But now… now…."

The Colonel held up his hands. I looked towards the southeast. Soldiers came riding toward us on horseback. Around me, the Indian children made a terrified chaos of screaming.

L.P. Delaney, Esq.

In the Colonel's tent a few hours later, the three of us sat talking, and the Colonel rejected every suggestion I made.

"With only two companies, ma'am? Why I wouldn't dare do it right now. And besides General Fleming'll be here by morning, so the best thing to do is to wait and see."

"Till morning!"

"I know you must be in a terrible state, Miss Rawlings. But the longer we wait, the more the Indians're liable to be starved out. So the best thing to do…"

"Please, please." And now I appealed to Delaney who sat silent in the tent, smoking. "If you'd only bring a wagonload of bread up to the edge of the oasis, and leave it there. Just one wagonload…"

"We simply can't do it, ma'am. For one thing, we're short on food ourselves, we're waiting right now for General Fleming to come. And it's him who has to have the final say where men's lives are to be risked."

"But by morning they may decide to move further north again. Or what if they come this way instead?"

"I'm thinking of that, Ma'am. That's why I've got us ringed like we are, and with the machine guns on our flanks. But if you'd just go ahead now, fill us in with as many details as you can remember…."

So I began talking. I told as much as I could recall, and all the while the Colonel took notes, and the Captain sat there, staring at me, his brown face lean and bronzed in the light of the portable oil lamp.

When I finished, the Colonel went out to check his sentries, and Delaney and myself were left staring at each other.

"No danger!" he said after a while and laughed.

"What?"

"I told you there was no danger, Ma'am. In the wagon, remember? When you were yelling to me about going back to Chadron..."

"Yes, God what a ninny I was, yelling like that. But it seems like ten years ago at least..."

We sat in silence. I could feel his dark eyes on me all the while.

"I guess I should apologize for something else too."

"Ma'am?"

"If I hadn't started yelling a little while ago, you wouldn't have shot off that flare. And then we wouldn't've been fired upon first..."

"Why Ma'am, it wasn't your fault."

"Oh the whole things seems so senseless to me! Those Indians praying for a miracle, a man like Running Bear turning his back on hope for help from the government, and hardly anybody caring to know the reasons why."

He didn't say anything. I heard the wind outside, and even though I was dead from lack of sleep, I couldn't sleep then, I had to keep on talking.

"Delaney..."

"Ma'am?"

"What do they do when they take somebody's scalp? Do they kill him first?"

"Now Ma'am, that's nothing to think about."

"Oh I know it's silly... But the way they were painting themselves, and the way he looked at me..."

"Other troops are coming up, ma'am. By morning, General Fleming'll be here."

"Before everything seemed so hopeless anyway, I just gave up I guess. And besides, Running Bear was my protection. But look at me – all of a sudden I'm so afraid my teeth are chattering. And that's just plain stupid, isn't it?"

He got up and came across to where I was, patting me on the shoulder for reassurance. And then suddenly – don't ask me how it happened – I found myself crying, womanlike, against his coat-buttons, his arms tight around me, his lips on my hair.

But it was only for half a moment. Because the Colonel came back, shivering with the cold, stamping fresh flakes off his cap.

"More snow," he said. "I don't think they'll leave the shelter of the oasis in this storm. But we'll just have to sit tight for a while and see..."

I went to another tent where the Indian children were, and bundled myself in army blankets. But I didn't sleep. I thought of Running Bear and the nightmare of the past several days, the futile grandeur and pity all mixed in together.

Then I began to think of Delaney.

Out of the Question

Loud voices were yelling and I opened my eyes and saw it was daylight. Around me, young Lakota faces were munching Army hardtack, their black eyes staring like so many wet olives. I went out and found the snow had stopped, at least three more inches must have fallen during the night, the drifts in some places were piled several feet high.

But there seemed to be a great many more soldiers about. I was conscious of bearded male grins, male eyes taking me in. Then I saw Colonel Donaldson, and with him another man, short bearded, and wearing two stars.

"Here she is, sir," the Colonel said, and both of them came over to me.

"By God," yelled the shorter one in a base voice, pumping my hand up and down, "that was a plucky thing to do, Mam. The Colonel's told me how you got away from those savages all by yourself, single-handed. You have my admiration, Mam."

"General, if you'll come to my tent for a minute," the Colonel began, but the General went right on, telling me how I was front page news, and it wasn't those filthy savages' fault that I hadn't starved to death, was it. But don't worry, he declared, the Army would guarantee me a safe trip back now. And had I been tortured? Of course he could well understand, he said, if there were some things I didn't want to talk about yet. But never mind, this time once and for all the hostiles would be put in their place.

The Colonel looked pained, and I kept my mouth shut. Then I saw Delaney over by the food wagons.

"Everyone's gone a little crazy," Delaney said. "They've shipped more troops out from Fort Garrison, and the General's been getting couriers to quell the insurrection at all costs, put down the rampaging Indians. People from Washington have come out too. He wants to march on the oasis right away…"

"Rampaging Indians!"

"Even when the Colonel told him what you told us, about what happened since they went off the reservation, he keeps answering: never mind, never mind, it's an insurrection in force. They've got to surrender before we decide what to do with them…"

"But that means that…"

"Miss Rawlings!"

It was Colonel Donaldson's voice, calling me to come to his tent. I went, and found the General pacing up and down inside, and when Donaldson asked me to repeat what I'd suggested the night before, about using bread as bait to convince the Indians peace and not retribution, was the Government's aim, I got all confused fearing the General might start yelling at me. But then another idea came to me suddenly. I got up, clenched my hands in front, began speaking in a halting, breathless voice.

When I finished, both men looked at each other.

"In the first place, the children'd be afraid to do it," the Colonel said. "Going out there like that alone..."

"Not alone..."

"But who should go out there with.... Oh no, that's absolutely out of the question, Ma'am. After all you've been through?"

"I absolutely forbid it!" the General yelled.

"But, sir," I said, and this time I forgot everything, how afraid I'd been the night before, and the suffering misery of the past few days, - everything except the useless slaughter that a full-scale battle would bring to both sides. "It's snowed again, and that means they're even more miserable and hungry, and if we walked right into their camp with bread to eat, bringing the children back with us...."

"No!" yelled the General. "Out of the question!"

"Please, sir..."

"Absolutely out of the question! Harebrained foolishness!"

"But General..."

"That's alright, Miss Rawlings," the Colonel said. "If you could leave us alone now for a while, because the General and I have some things to talk over, why we'll call you if there's anything else you might be able to help us with."

Delaney was waiting for me when I went out. We went into the children's tent alone for a while, talked. Then we heard

Donaldson calling my name again, and when we went out, there he was, and the General with him, and we could see by the look on Donaldson's face that the General had been convinced.

Delaney's fingers pressed against mine.

The Worst One of All

"Keep walking," the Colonel said. "Never mind those guns..."

"Stay behind me," Delaney said. The three of us together with three Indian military scouts, and the group of Sioux children, were approaching the oasis. We had gotten down, were coming on foot to make our peaceful purposes absolutely clear. Colonel Donaldson was leading the team of horses by the reins, and, in back, that wagonload of bread and dried meat and Army blankets, and shoes, squished and slid through the snow.

We came to where the Indian lookouts were. They were hostile, menacing us with guns, shouting in Lakota tongue. We stopped and Colonel Donaldson answered back, and then the Indian kids as I'd told them to, clambered down from the wagon and went forward with loaves of bread in their hands.

We watched, waiting. We saw them take the loaves and break them into pieces, wolfing the bread hungrily. We started forward again, the Colonel talking all the time. When we came up to where they were, and they saw that no one in our party was carrying a gun, they held out their hands for more bread, letting us pass.

We went into the oasis.

A pitiful sight, Delaney and the Colonel were stunned to see... From all sides, skeletons of old woman, children, bloody and barefoot in the snow, wraith-like old men, came up to the wagon, clamoring, holding out their hands, and the Colonel was busy handing out food and blankets, talking all the time while Delaney and I helped him. And then we saw Running Bear, his blanket pulled tight around, standing a little ways off, and watching us with pain and disillusion. He had told the people we were coming to kill them, the young men had painted themselves for a death battle, and here we came with food and blankets...

Little by little, the painted warriors edged forward, put down their guns. And in their misery and need they stretched out their hands....

I saw Black Pony and a few of his followers standing to one side, hostile, despising the rabble of petitioners. But then the Colonel stood up in the wagon, and talked finally to Running Bear, saying more wagons full of more food and supplies were waiting outside, and the American General also was there, but that if the people consented to come peacefully back to the land they had left, under escort of the Army, no one would be hurt, they would be fed and sheltered. Running Bear looked long at the ragged cohort all around. Then he looked to where we were, and his eyes were stricken. Then he unbuckled his rifle in a gesture of surrender, and put it down in the snow beside him.

There was a great shout. The people began clamoring for food, the young men removed their war feathers. I saw Black Pony come up to where Running Bear was and shout at him angrily, and spit in the snow, a gesture of contempt. But there was no response. They tried to provoke him into a fight, but he stood impassive, listening to their taunts. And when they tore his war feathers away, he made no move to resist...

So that was how it was when the Army moved up into the oasis, after we sent a scout back with the Colonel's note. Tipis frozen in the snow; Indians massed, waiting for more food and blankets; soldiers moving into the area with drawn rifles, and the General himself riding up with his rifle across his saddle.

But the food wagons were left outside. No one was bringing them up yet and Colonel Donaldson went over to where General Fleming sat, surveying the scene.

"I told them we'd issue rations right away, sir. So if those wagons could be brought up..."

"No! Not until they've surrendered to Army authority," said General Fleming, and glared at the mass of faces.

"But my God, they've given in, General. You can see the condition they're in. So if you could order the wagons to be brought up...."

"I want their arms, Colonel. Tell them to turn in their rifles, and then we'll talk about issuance of rations..."

"But I promised them, sir, that food would be given right away. And you can see for yourself how..."

"That's alright. I'm not going to take any more chances. You tell them to turn in their arms."

"Sir, I don't think that's a wise thing right now to..."

"Never mind, never mind. You just translate what I said..."

We sat there on the wagon and the Colonel got up while the Indians looked at the companies of soldiers, standing all around, and after he finished speaking, there was a sudden silence, a tension in the air. A few Indians, old men mostly, came forward and laid their rifles in the snow. But the rest just stood and looked around at the guns and massed soldiers. My own throat was parched, I moved closer to Delaney...

"What is this, a joke, Colonel?" General Fleming cried. "I asked for their arms."

"Please, General, if you'll only bring the food up..."

"Goddammit! They're not getting any more food until we've disarmed them! I've had enough of Indian trickery in this part of the country. Now you tell them that, and tell them if they don't turn in every last rifle, pronto, we'll search every last tipi in the place, so help me."

The Colonel looked tired and said a few words, but no one moved. Ugliness was in the air suddenly. Then the General gave an order for soldiers to begin searching the hutments for guns, and a low singing chant began among the massed Sioux. The next second the most awful few minutes in my life began.

I think it was Black Pony who fired the first shot, but I'm not sure because the whole place just shuddered into violence. Whether it came from a Sioux, or a nervous soldier somewhere who felt an attack coming, that one bullet was like a match touched to an unspeakable explosive, buried in the middle of a mass of desperate people.

General Fleming shouted an order, and I saw the Colonel jump up, shaking his head, trying to countermand the firing of a Hotchkiss gun set up on the flank of the encampment. But it was already too late. I saw the Colonel fall down dead, shot through the throat, and heard an awful screaming and guns firing and soldiers crying about remembering Custer, and Indians screaming war yells, and luckily I fainted dead away....

When I came to, I found myself on a kind of hillock south of the encampment, blood falling on me, and a single Indian with a rifle crouched nearby in the snow.

From somewhere half-way up the hillock, somebody was shouting my name.

"Miss Rawlings..... Miss Rawlings...."

Running Bear turned and looked at me. His shoulder was torn he was naked from the waist up. I couldn't open my mouth to say a word. Later on, I learned how he'd caught me up from the wagon when I fell in the melee, and had fled with me up here, probably saving my life, and Delaney's to boot. Because the Captain had rushed out of the center of the holocaust, following us up here, and now I recognized his voice suddenly, half-way up the slope, shouting out again:

"Miss Rawlings..... Miss Rawlings......" And then: "Can you hear me?...." And then: "Shout, say something, I don't care what just so long as I know you can hear. Because otherwise I'm going to come up this slope and I swear to God..."

Like a kind of nightmare it seemed, and how could Delaney have known what was going on above? All he heard was that one shot, and me screaming afterwards, and then he came rampaging up to find me crying wildly, kneeling in the snow beside that dead Indian, shot through the heart by his own hand.

Which was how the soldiers found us. They came running up the hill soon after, pouring fusillade after fusillade into Running Bear's dead body. And the General himself came too, puffing his way up to where we were.

"By God, I told Donaldson a hundred times he was wrong. Always making a million excuses, and all he got was a slug through his throat for his pains. But it'll be the last time they'll try anything like this. Because I had my son deployed, guns in place; we were ready for once...."

And gazing down to where the dead man lay. "Good riddance! Pretending to be loyal to the Army and all that time plotting the worst trouble on the whole reservation. The worst one of all…"

Then he asked if there was anything he could do for me, and I told him no thanks. Down below we could hear an awful moaning for the grieved and wounded, and soldiers swearing, old women singing their mourning chants, children crying in the cold. But no firing. The holocaust was over.

When the General left, Delaney and myself stood over the body on the hillock, not saying a word; we stayed up there a long time.

Promised Land

Flags, bunting, - they had the whole main street of Rushville decked out in festive banners, you might've thought it was a holiday of some kind! And people shooting firecrackers off, visiting dignitaries, newspapermen, speechmaking. Even a congressman was there, though I forgot his name. But I know what he said. "Courageous example of fortitude," and "inspiration to thousands." Also, "shining reflection of what faith can do to bring you through tribulations beyond description."

I remember how he ended his speech too. "Let us hope that the gallant victory of General Fleming will be the last chapter of violence on the Indian frontier, and that the memories of the martyred, both Indian and white, may serve as a sober reminder in days to come of our government's refusal to countenance insurrection from whoever quarter it may come. And let us also pray for wisdom and understanding to solve peacefully all the manifold aspects of the Indian problem that yet remain before us...."

But I guess it was the newspaperman who bothered me the most, always following me around, wanting to take a million pictures. And when they found out about Delaney and me, trying to get us to sign a paper for our true-life love story.

But it was General Fleming who'll probably remember that day more than anybody else. Because there he was, army officers from Washington on both sides of him, talking about a posthumous medal for Colonel Donaldson, and a citation for all of us, giving generous credit to his men, being very humble about it all. Then somebody called up Delaney to speak a few words.

He looked pale on the wooden platform, with the townspeople thronged around, the dignitaries sitting in a row, the sun slanting on his face.

"What I have to say isn't much," Delaney began, "only I don't think anyone'll care to hear it. I sit here listening to talk about the great victory, and how this should be a lesson for lawlessness in the future, and I'll tell you what I think."

"I think it's all a bunch of lies! What victory? The Indians were murdered in cold blood, plain and simple. And before that they were killed too, only the killing took a lot of time, a number of years. There are plenty of ways to kill a man. You don't have to take a bunch of soldiers and Gatling guns like General Fleming, and blunder into a wholesale butchery to satisfy the panic of a lot of scared loudmouths."

"But it's not only them who're to blame. Everyone is! I'd like to ask who really knows the Indians. Does anyone really deep down care what they're like, or how their life is, or what's happening to their own respect for themselves? Not more'n a dozen in this town ever took the trouble to learn to speak with an Indian in his own language. Now General Fleming spoke of a memorial for Colonel Donaldson, and I say that's hypocrisy. Sure, the Colonel was a good man, not many like him, but I say that the man who gave me this knife was also a good man, a better man than anybody on this platform right now, and he was an Indian, the same one we've all been thanking God is rotting away today in the filthy desert."

"I don't care to make you a speech, I'm not much on that. Only I just want to say right out that I feel filthy today, and as citizens of this county, so should you. Because something's happening out there on the frontier that stinks, it smells to high heaven, and it's more important than anybody's treatment of the Indians. More important because it concerns the whole country, the children and grandchildren of everybody listening to me today."

"Now in 50 years there probably won't be any frontier left, as we know it. Only one great country and men running it that came some of them from frontiersmen like yourselves. Well, I say that if all they've learned is what we're learning right now about understanding strangers, or if all they want is what we want, more of what we can touch with our hands and fingers, the country'll be great and powerful and all that, but I say it really won't amount to much."

"A little while ago, General Fleming was kind enough to talk about a promotion for me, or a citation, but I've decided to resign my commission anyway, so there's no need for anyone to bother with anything like that. Not that I have anything against the army, I don't blame the army for anything. Only I just discovered something else I'd rather do for a while. So thanks very much just the same."

"I told you this wasn't going to be such a hot speech, didn't I?"

He came down from the platform, and there was silence all around, a kind of stunned shock. Oh I loved that Delaney then! He saw me smiling at him, and he came towards me and we walked down the street, and hitched a buggy up, and rode off towards the Sioux relief encampment at Forked River. And right then the sun was shining all around – glittering on rocks, hills, trees, bluffs where the Indians still lived, grouped together in hunger and despair, waiting for time when sympathy on our part and forgiveness on theirs might make it possible for the old prophecies to be realized; allowing the nation to walk erect, transforming through work and love the very ground under their feet into a place of food, warmth, strength, and self-respect again: the dream incarnate of the promised land!

EPITAPH

From chapter three, ("Hunters Across the Prairie")

Of Erick Erickson's book, *Childhood and Society*, published by Norton in 1950:

"The Sioux tribe as a whole is still waiting

for the Supreme Court to give the Black Hills

back to them and to restore the lost buffalo......"

66483888R00075

Made in the USA
Charleston, SC
20 January 2017